Stacey's Ex-Best Friend

**Other books by
Ann M. Martin**

*Rachel Parker, Kindergarten Show-off
Eleven Kids, One Summer
Ma and Pa Dracula
Yours Turly, Shirley
Ten Kids, No Pets
Slam Book
Just a Summer Romance
Missing Since Monday
With You and Without You
Me and Katie (the Pest)
Stage Fright
Inside Out
Bummer Summer*

BABY-SITTERS LITTLE SISTER series
THE BABY-SITTERS CLUB mysteries
THE BABY-SITTERS CLUB series

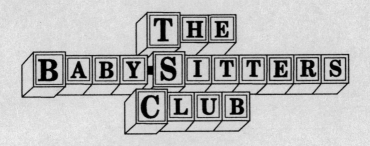

Stacey's Ex-Best Friend

Ann M. Martin

AN
APPLE
PAPERBACK

SCHOLASTIC INC.
New York Toronto London Auckland Sydney

Cover art by Hodges Soileau

No part of this publication may be reproduced in whole or in part, or stored in a retrieval system, or transmitted in any form or by any means, electronic, mechanical, photocopying, recording, or otherwise, without written permission of the publisher. For information regarding permission, write to Scholastic Inc., 555 Broadway, New York, NY 10012.

ISBN 0-590-92574-1

12 11 10 9 8 7 6 5 4 3 2   9   7 8 9/9 0 1/0

Printed in the U.S.A.   40

For Gemma and Hallie

CHAPTER 1

Snow was falling again.

For a planet that's supposed to be feeling the effects of global warming, it certainly was having a cold winter. And a snowy one. That was okay with me. I like snow. It makes me feel cozy. Now that my mom and I live in a real house in the country and have an actual working fireplace, the coziness is even better. Last week when it was snowing (for, like, the seventy-fifth time since the beginning of January), Mom and I made popcorn after supper and ate it in front of the fire. No TV, no radio or music, just Mom and me and the popcorn and the fireplace.

Does that sound lonely? Well, it wasn't. It was peaceful and wonderful. But I have to tell you that my family used to be bigger. That was when my parents were living together. But a few months ago they got divorced. Mom and I moved here to Stoneybrook, Connecti-

1

cut. Oh, all right, we don't actually live in the *country*. We live in a small town. But Stoneybrook sure feels like the country compared to New York City, which is where I grew up. And where my father still lives.

My name is Stacey McGill. I'm thirteen. I'm an only child. And I am now officially a divorced kid. As I said, I grew up in New York, the Big Apple. I was born there, and I love that city. Really. I love everything about it. Well, almost everything. I don't love rats, of course. Or cockroaches. Or crime or guns or violence. But I do love the museums and the historical landmarks and the stores and theaters and restaurants. And the tall buildings. And the hidden pockets of surprise—tiny parks and old houses and gardens that you find just by turning a corner, and that are not mentioned in any guidebook. (Can you tell I ♥ good old NYC?)

Okay, so I was born in the city, and Mom and Dad and I lived there until the company Dad works for changed his job and we had to relocate to Connecticut. That was at the beginning of seventh grade. I am now an eighth-grader at Stoneybrook Middle School (SMS). But I haven't lived solely in Connecticut during the past year. No, that would be too simple. Here's the thing: We'd been living in Stoneybrook for just under a year (long enough for me to adjust to small-town life and to make a group of really good friends, including a new best friend), when Dad's company transferred him back to New York. So we picked up and moved again. I returned to my old life. A new apartment, but the same private school, the same NYC neighborhood, and my *other* best friend, my New York best friend, Laine Cummings.

And then it happened. Something I'd been afraid of for a few years, ever since the parents of several of my friends started getting divorced. My own parents began to fight. And finally they made The Announcement. *They* were getting divorced. To make things even more complicated, Dad decided to stay in New York (he would move to a small apartment, though), while Mom wanted to return to Stoneybrook. *I* had to choose where I wanted to live. In other words, I had to choose between my parents. After a lot of thinking (and a lot of crying and apologizing), I decided to go back to Connecticut. But I made my parents promise I could visit Dad in New York a *lot*. They promised. So here I am in Stoneybrook, in a little house with Mom.

Why did I decide to live in Connecticut instead of in the Big Apple? Mostly because I have so many friends here. The first time I moved to Stoneybrook I joined the Baby-sitters

Club (BSC). (I'll explain that later.) The club is made up of seven members: me and six other SMS students. Those six students are my good friends. And one of them, Claudia Kishi, is the new best friend I mentioned.

I do miss Dad and New York and Laine Cummings, but they're just a train ride away, which isn't bad.

That snowy afternoon was on a Wednesday. My friends and I were going to hold a BSC meeting, but it wouldn't start for two hours, so I decided to begin my homework. Often on weekday afternoons I'm busy with a baby-sitting job. But not that day.

I pulled out my math book. I just adore math. (Honest. I really do.) Before I had even opened the book, though, the phone rang. I dashed into Mom's room and picked up the upstairs extension.

"Hello?" I said.

"Hey, Anastasia! It's me!"

"Laine!" I cried. "Hi. . . . Why are you calling me Anastasia?"

"I don't know. I guess it's just more grown-up than Stacey."

"I guess," I replied. I pictured Laine. She was probably curled up in the armchair next to her phone. (Note that I said *her* phone. She has a private line and everything. Well, so does Claud, my other best friend.)

"How's it going?" asked Laine.

"Fine. How are you doing?"

"I'm great! All I can think about is our winter break. It's coming up, you know. One week surrounded by two weekends. Nine glorious days of freedom, from Saturday, February seventh, through Sunday, February fifteenth. I absolutely cannot wait."

I smiled. Vacations have always been important to Laine. And since my parents are good friends of her parents, we've taken some vacations together. I mean, our families have.

"What are you going to do during those nine glorious days?" I asked.

Laine sighed. "I have so many choices," she said.

"Poor baby."

Laine laughed. "Let's see. What I *think* I'm going to do is just stay here. There'll be a ton of good parties to go to. And King will be here. We'll go to the parties together. King is really tight with my friends. The age difference doesn't seem to matter at all. You know."

I didn't know. Laine and I are close, but it's not like we talk every day, the way we did when we were going to the same school. "Um . . . what do you mean? About the age difference?" I asked.

"Well, King is fifteen. Didn't I mention that?"

"No." The last time we had spoken was on New Year's Eve. I was sure I would have remembered if Laine had told me about a fifteen-year-old boyfriend named King. You don't forget a name—or an age—like that. "I don't think you mentioned King at all," I told Laine.

"Oh. Well, he goes to Rudy Matthews School. Across the street." (Laine meant across the street from her school.) "I met him at this party. His hair is kind of long and he wears it in a ponytail, which I think is awesome. Anyway, we've been going out for two weeks now. We can't wait for vacation. He'll be on vacation when I am. And a lot of *his* friends will be throwing parties, so I'll be hanging around with the high-school crowd, more or less."

Gosh. An older boyfriend named King. High-school kids. I was amazed.

"But," Laine went on, "I could also go on our school's ski trip. Or I could fly (by myself, of course) to Florida and stay at Aunt Mona and Uncle Edgar's condo. It's right on the beach."

Suddenly I had a brilliant thought. It just flashed into my head out of nowhere. "Hey!" I cried. "I've got a better idea. You could come *here!* You could spend your vacation in Sto-neybrook. Wouldn't that be terrific? I wouldn't be on vacation, but that would be okay. Claud and everyone would be around. And you've never been here. You haven't seen my house or the town or my school. You'd like to see my friends again, wouldn't you?" (Laine has met the members of the BSC several times.) "Maybe you could come to school with us. Oh, and meet the kids we baby-sit for. Laine, this would be so distant!"

"It would be so *what*?"

"So distant. Oh, I forgot. My friends and I made up that word. It means, you know, like really, *really* cool."

"Oh." Laine paused. Then she said, "Stace, I don't know."

"You *have* to come, Laine. Please, please, please?" I stopped, realizing I sounded like a little kid. And also realizing I should mention my brilliant idea to Mom before Laine accepted the invitation. "Laine?" I said. "Think about it, okay? I'm going to get permission from Mom. I'll call you back around five. Before our BSC meeting."

Well, I got permission from Mom in a snap. No problem. As I said, she and Laine's mom are really good friends. Mom has known Laine since the day Laine was born, and she adores her. She thinks she's wonderful. So the idea of a week-long visit from Laine was just fine with my mother.

When I called Laine back (on the *dot* of five o'clock) the first thing I said was, "It's all set. I got permission. You can come!"

"Okay . . ." replied Laine, slowly.

"Okay, you'll come?" I exclaimed. "That's fantastic! How will I ever wait until February seventh? It feels like it's years away."

I chattered on until Laine said, "Don't you have to go to a BSC meeting or something?"

"Yeah, you're right. I better get off the phone. But I'll call you in a few days so we can make plans. Talk to you then. 'Bye, Laine!"

I hung up the phone. But since I didn't have to leave immediately for our club meeting, I began making a list of things Laine would enjoy doing in Stoneybrook. She could spend a day at school. She could come on a baby-sitting job with me. Maybe she would meet Charlotte Johanssen, who's my favorite kid to sit for. We could go shopping. We could go to a movie. It was too bad there aren't a lot of good restaurants here. Laine likes to eat. In New York she can choose from thousands of restaurants. But not here.

Where I'm concerned, maybe that's lucky. See, I have to be careful about what I eat. I stick to a pretty strict diet. This is because I have diabetes. I'm what's called a brittle diabetic, which means I have a severe form of the disease. A diabetic can't process sugar the way most people can. So I have to stay away from desserts and sweets (I can eat fruit, though) and also give *myself* injections of something called insulin. And I have to test the level of sugar in my blood every day. Too high or too low and I could get really sick. Needless to say, eating isn't exactly my hobby.

It's funny about insulin and food and Laine. Laine and I had our most memorable fight several years ago when I first got sick. Laine did not understand about diabetes at all. She just thought my sickness was gross, if not contagious. (Which it isn't.) Oh, well. Eventually we made up. And we've made up after our other fights, too. That's how some friendships work. You fight, you make up, you fight, you make up.

I bounced out of my room. Time for the meeting of the Baby-sitters Club. And time to see my other best friend.

CHAPTER 2

I knew Claudia would be happy to hear about Laine's trip to Stoneybrook. As I mentioned, Laine has met my friends in the Baby-sitters Club several times. That's because most of the BSC members have been to New York several times. And *that's* because my friends and I do a lot of things together. I mean, aside from attending club meetings.

One of the many things I like about the BSC is that we're a great group of friends. Sometimes I think that's even more important than the fact that we're a successful baby-sitting business. Although that's certainly important, too. The BSC was the idea of Kristy Thomas. She's the club president now. It was Kristy who thought of turning baby-sitting into a business. This was her simple but brilliant reasoning: when a parent needs a sitter, he or she could save time finding one by placing a single phone call and reaching a whole group of sitters at once. One club member would surely be free, so the parent could line up a sitter without having to make any more calls.

The BSC started out with just four members: Kristy, Claudia Kishi, Mary Anne Spier, and me. Soon we needed another member, so Dawn Schafer joined the club. Finally Jessi Ramsey and Mallory Pike (eleven-year-old sixth-graders) also joined. Now the seven of us meet three times a week, on Monday, Wednesday, and Friday afternoons from five-thirty until six. Parents know they can call us during those times and reach seven capable sitters. How do they know when to call us? Because we advertise. We've handed out fliers and even placed an ad in the local paper. Business is booming!

The club is successful for a number of reasons. I think the main one is that Kristy runs it in such a businesslike, professional manner. Every member of the club has a title, and most of us have specific responsibilities, too. Claud is the vice-president, Mary Anne is the secretary, I'm the treasurer, and Dawn is what we call the alternate officer. Jessi and Mal are junior officers. Before you see the club members in action, let me tell you a little about each of them, their lives and the roles they play in the club.

As president, Kristy does more than run the

club. She also keeps coming up with her great ideas. She's famous for them. One was the BSC notebook. Long ago (okay, last year, when most of us were twelve and in seventh grade) Kristy thought that keeping a sort of diary of our baby-sitting jobs would be helpful. So now after any of us goes on a job, that sitter is responsible for writing it up in the notebook. Then once a week we're supposed to read the notebook to find out what happened when our friends were sitting, how they solved baby-sitting problems, and what's going on in the lives of kids we might sit for soon ourselves.

Another of Kristy's ideas was the BSC record book. We find that keeping records is important to the business. In the record book are listed our clients — their addresses and phone numbers, the rates they pay, and the ages of their children. Also in the record book are the scheduling pages where we keep track of the jobs we've signed up for.

Then there are Kid-Kits. As far as children are concerned, Kid-Kits were Kristy's all-time greatest idea. Each of us sitters has a Kid-Kit, which is simply a cardboard box decorated with paint and glitter and filled with child-appealing stuff — our old toys, games, and books, plus art supplies, activity books, and so forth. We sometimes bring the kits with us

12

when we baby-sit, and our charges adore them. Which is great. Happy kids mean happy parents who will want to call the BSC with future sitting jobs! What on earth would the club do without Kristy?

Kristy has a very interesting family. She lives with her mom; her stepfather; her three brothers (Sam and Charlie, who are in high school, and David Michael, who's just seven); her grandmother; her adopted sister, Emily Michelle, who's two and a half; and (part-time) her stepsister and stepbrother, Karen and Andrew, who are seven and four. Before Kristy's mom met Watson (Kristy's stepfather), the Thomases lived in a modest house across the street from Claud. Then Watson came into their lives and whisked them into his mansion on the other side of town. (Watson is a millionaire.)

Kristy's life changed completely, but I think she's adjusted to everything, including Watson. Kristy is a very strong person. (Actually, she can be maddeningly stubborn.) She's outgoing, she likes to talk, and she's always coming up with great ideas. Kristy is also sort of a tomboy. She loves sports, and we rarely see her dressed in anything but jeans, a turtleneck shirt, running shoes, and maybe a sweater and her baseball cap. Just for the fun of it, she coaches a softball team for little kids in Stoneybrook. Her team is called Kristy's Krushers. An opposing team is Bart's Bashers, and guess what. Kristy and Bart Taylor have started going to dances and stuff. I guess you could call them girlfriend and boyfriend. (But don't let Kristy hear you!) Kristy is short, the shortest in our class, and she has shoulder-length brown hair and deep brown eyes.

Kristy's best friend is Mary Anne Spier, the secretary of the BSC. Mary Anne has quite a job! She's the one who has to keep the BSC record book in order, which means she's in charge of scheduling all jobs. And *that* means she has to be familiar with a lot of complicated lives. She has to know when Kristy is holding Krushers practices, when Claudia is going to art lessons, or Jessi is taking ballet classes, or when Mallory has to go to the orthodontist. Mary Anne is neat and precise and accurate, so she's perfect for the job.

What sort of personality would you expect from the best friend of Kristy Thomas? One as outgoing and as free-spirited as Kristy's? Well, that's not Mary Anne. She and Kristy may be close, but Mary Anne is shy, quiet, unsure of herself, and a big romantic. Also, she cries really easily. Just mention *Gone With the Wind* or *Love Story*, and Mary Anne's eyes turn into leaky faucets. Maybe it's fitting that

Mary Anne was the first of us BSC members to have a steady boyfriend.

Considering how different Mary Anne and Kristy are, it's interesting that they actually look sort of alike. Mary Anne is also short (not quite as short as Kristy, though), and has brown hair and brown eyes. However, she wears glasses for reading. And she cares about clothes. Her strictish father won't let her wear anything too trendy, but at least Mary Anne can get away with bright colors, baggy tops, and a fair amount of jewelry.

Mary Anne lives with her dad, her stepmother, and her stepsister. (Her mom died a long time ago.) Believe it or not, her stepsister is . . . Dawn Schafer, who happens to be Mary Anne's other best friend. (Mary Anne's like me; she has two best friends.) Can you imagine being best friends and then winding up as stepsisters? I can't. Although, I guess I might have a stepsister of my own one day. Who knows what would happen if Mom or Dad got married again? Anyway, Mary Anne, her dad, and her kitten, Tigger, moved into Dawn's colonial farmhouse not long ago, and Mary Anne likes being part of a bigger family for the first time in her life.

Okay. You've met several pairs of best friends. Now it's time for you to meet my

Stoneybrook best friend, Claudia Kishi. Claud is the BSC vice-president mainly because we hold our meetings in her room. This means invading her room three times a week, eating her junk food, and tying up her phone. Like Laine, Claud has her own phone and her own phone number. This is primarily why we chose her room as the BSC headquarters. We can use her phone during meetings and not have to worry that someone else is waiting (impatiently) to talk on it.

Claud was born and raised here in Stoneybrook. She lives with her mom and dad and her older sister, Janine. She's an incredibly talented artist. She can sculpt, draw, paint, even make jewelry. Unfortunately, she is not a wonderful student. She could be, if she wanted, since she's smart. But school doesn't interest her much.

Claud has two addictions that she tries to keep secret from her parents: junk food and Nancy Drew mysteries. Her parents don't approve of either, so Claud hides stuff all around her room. Lift up her pillow and there's a Snickers bar. Look in the back of a desk drawer and there's a bag of Fritos. Search through the mess on the floor of her closet and there's *The Clue of the Tapping Heels*. Claud is such a character.

I wish you could *see* Claudia Kishi. She's

absolutely beautiful. And exotic. She's Japanese-American. Her hair is silky and black and *long*. And her eyes are dark and almond-shaped. She's tall and thin and a very distant dresser. Claud cares about clothes as much as Kristy *doesn't* care about them. That's one thing Claud and I have in common. If I may say so, we are pretty sophisticated. We both like wild outfits — leggings, cowboy boots, short skirts, the layered look, cool hats. And we pay a lot of attention to our nails and our makeup and especially to our hair. I am constantly getting my hair permed. (My hair is blonde and wavy; the perm makes it look even wavier.) Claud likes to experiment with different hairstyles. And she likes hair ornaments — beads and ponytail ties and flowers. You know what's kind of funny? Claudia and I are both a little boy-crazy. That's safe to say. But neither of us has had a steady boyfriend. (Sigh.)

While I'm on the subject of me, I'll tell you about my role in the BSC. As treasurer, I'm the one who collects club dues from everybody at our Monday meetings. Since I like math, I'm good at keeping track of the money in our treasury. I dole out the funds as they're needed, usually to buy supplies for the Kid-Kits, to pay Kristy's brother Charlie to drive her to and from meetings now that she lives across town, and to help Claudia pay her phone bill.

We decided to make Dawn our alternate officer. (Well, Kristy thought of the idea, of course.) The alternate officer is supposed to be able to take over for any member of the club who can't make a meeting. This doesn't happen often. (I mean, we don't miss meetings often.) Even so, Dawn has to be familiar with the duties of the president, the vice-president, the secretary, and the treasurer. So far, she's done a terrific job.

Like me, Dawn was not born and raised in Stoneybrook. She moved here in the middle of seventh grade. All the way from California. Her parents were getting a divorce, and her mom wanted to live in the town in which she'd grown up. So she moved Dawn and her younger brother, Jeff, clear across the country. The move was difficult, but Dawn and her mother adjusted. Jeff did not, though, and finally he moved back to California to live with his father. He's happier there. Dawn misses him, of course, but she's happier now, too — ever since her mom married Mary Anne's dad. Overnight she acquired a second family.

Dawn's pretty easygoing. Maybe that's one reason Mary Anne likes her. She's also fairly self-confident and very much an individual. Mostly, she does what she wants without worrying what others will think of her. (She isn't thoughtless, though. Just sure of herself.) Dawn is pretty. She's slender with bright blue eyes, a few freckles, and very long, straw-colored hair. She dresses in her own style, casual but trendy. (I think she dresses for comfort as well as for looks.)

Now, don't worry. I haven't forgotten about the two junior members of the BSC, Mal and Jessi. (They're the ones who are eleven and in sixth grade.) "Junior member" means they're younger and their parents don't allow them to baby-sit at night, unless they're watching their own brothers and sisters. Mostly, they sit after school and on weekend days.

Jessi and Mal are excellent baby-sitters. They ought to be. Each of them has younger brothers and sisters. That's an understatement for Mallory. She has *seven* younger brothers and sisters. (Jessi has one younger sister and a baby brother.)

Mal and Jessi have a lot in common, which is nice, considering they're best friends. Both of them wish their parents would let them grow up faster. And both of them *adore* reading, especially horse stories. Mal also likes mysteries. But they have separate interests, as well. Jessi is a dancer, a ballerina. She's extremely talented and has danced onstage in lots of productions. Mallory is a writer, an aspiring author. She hopes to write children's books someday. Maybe she'll illustrate them, too.

Jessi and Mal do not look a thing alike. Jessi has chocolatey brown skin, dark eyes, black hair, and does not wear glasses. Mal has pale skin, blue eyes, unruly red hair, and she does wear glasses. Her parents say she is too young for contacts. At least they caved in and let Mal get her ears pierced. (Jessi's parents did the same thing.)

I looked around Claud's room. The time was 5:25, according to her digital clock (which is the official club timepiece). The seven main members of the BSC had arrived. (I should mention that two other people belong to the club, but they don't attend meetings. They are associate members, reliable sitters we can call on just in *case* someone phones in with a job that none of us is available to take. Guess who one of the associate members is. Mary Anne's boyfriend — Logan Bruno. The other is Shannon Kilbourne, a friend of Kristy's in her new neighborhood.)

We were sitting in our usual spots. Mal and Jessi were cross-legged on the floor, leaning against Claud's bed. Mary Anne, Claudia, and I were lined up *on* the bed, leaning against the wall. Dawn was straddling Claud's wooden desk chair backward, her chin resting on the top rung. She was chewing on the end of a Bic pen. Then there was Kristy. Our president sat regally in Claudia's director's chair. As always, a visor was perched on her head and a pencil was stuck over one ear. She was looking impatiently at the clock, waiting for five-thirty.

"Hey, everyone," I said. "I'm glad you're here early. Guess what."

"What," replied Jessi, her mouth full of gum. She craned her neck around and looked up at me. (She and Mal were working on another in a series of gum-wrapper chains.)

"In a couple of weeks we're going to have a visitor."

"*We* are?" said Claudia. She stopped braiding her hair.

"Well, sort of. I just got off the phone with Laine."

I told my friends about Laine's visit.

"Distant!" exclaimed Mallory. "I can't wait to see her again."

"Hey, she'll be here for the Valentine Dance," said Mary Anne. "Won't she? That's on the night of Friday the thirteenth." She paused. Then, "Oh, *ew!* The dance is going to be on *Friday the thirteenth?* Who planned that?"

"Our teachers, who else?" said Kristy.

"The Valentine Dance! I hadn't thought of that," I said. "Fresh. She'll be here for Valentine's Day, too, then. That'll be fun."

Mallory cleared her throat. She put down her end of the gum chain. "Um, I have a small announcement to make," she said. "Ben asked me to the dance."

In all honesty, this came as no great shock to me. Ben Hobart (who lives right across the street from Claud, in Mary Anne's old house) had taken Mal to our school's last big bash, the Winter Wonderland Dance. When you're eleven, though, I guess you don't expect relationships to last very long.

"That's great, Mal," said Kristy. "Bart's taking me."

"Logan's taking me," Mary Anne spoke up.

"Surprise, surprise," Dawn said, and giggled.

As it turned out, we had *all* been invited to the dance. Dawn and Claud and I were going with guys who are just friends of ours. Jessi was going with a seventh-grade boy. She sounded unreasonably excited whenever she said his name, Curtis Shaller. Maybe she was excited because a seventh-grader is an *older boy*. Or maybe she was just relieved to be going to the dance at all, considering that Quint, her real boyfriend, lives in New York City and wouldn't be able to take her. Or *maybe* —

"Order, please!" cried Kristy, and I nearly jumped out of my skin.

The meeting was beginning.

It was a fairly normal meeting. I say "fairly" because an out-of-the-ordinary thing did happen. Kristy had one of her flashes of brilliance — a great idea. She gets plenty of great ideas, as I've said, but she doesn't get one at *every* meeting. In the middle of phone calls and scheduling and talking about our sitting charges, Kristy jumped to her feet. "Oh, my gosh! I just got a terrific idea!" she exclaimed. "Valentine's Day is on Saturday this year. Why don't we give a Valentine party for a bunch of the kids we know? I bet they'd love it. They could exchange cards, and we could buy some of those candy conversation hearts . . ."

Kristy was off and running. Of course, her idea *was* terrific. A party would be great publicity for the club. More important, the kids would have fun.

What a day it had been!

Saturday

Oh, a rainy day at the Pikes' house.

Hey, don't groan, Stacey. Remember who you're with. Me, Mallory. One of the Pikes. And I wasn't

(In case you couldn't tell, I just grabbed the pen away from Mallory.) Of course I didn't mean Mal was part of the problem. Everyone got that, you guys?

Are you saying that my brothers and sisters are a problem?

NO! For heaven's sake. All right. I'm going to start again. Okay, it was a gorgeous rainy Saturday. Mal and I were sitting for Mal's charming younger brothers and sisters.... Mal, does this meet with your approval?

Yes, thank you.

The Pike kids. Mal is the oldest of eight, remember? And I'm an only child. Even though I've spent lots of time at the Pikes', I have difficulty imagining how it would feel to live in a house so full of people.

Let me introduce you to the rest of the Pikes: Claire is five and she's the baby of the family. She can be very silly at times. Margo is seven. She and Claire are best friends. Having your best friend right in your family must be awfully nice. Claire and Margo are lucky. (So are Mary Anne and Dawn.) Anyway, next in the Pike family is Nicky, who's eight. Sometimes Nicky feels a little left out of things. His brothers are older and don't always let him hang around with them, and Nicky does not like getting stuck with a "bunch of girls" — his words. Nicky is a good kid, though, and he has lots of friends in the neighborhood. Vanessa is nine years old and the family poet. (Writing must be in the Pike genes.) She's usually far-off and dreamy. Now. Maybe you're wondering. How can there be eight Pike kids, the oldest eleven and the youngest five, and space to squeeze in only one more kid between Vanessa and Mallory? Good question. The answer is there are three ten-year-old Pikes — identical triplets! Their names are Jordan, Adam, and Byron. What a household.

My sitting job with Mallory took place exactly one week and one day after my idea to invite Laine to Stoneybrook for her vacation. Since then, the plans for the BSC Valentine's Day party had really taken shape. We were going to call our party the Valentine Masquerade. This is why.

"In the olden days," said Jessi at our Monday club meeting, "didn't people used to send valentines without their names on them? You know, unsigned? Like, the card would read 'Happy Valentine's Day, my dearest darling sweetheart. All my love, guess who.' "

We laughed, and Mary Anne said. "I don't know, but that gives me an idea. What if, at the party, the kids exchanged cards and signed their names in code? We could tell the kids ahead of time who the other guests were going to be, and then they could make a card for each one. That would give them something fun to do the week of Valentine's Day. You know how zooey they get before a holiday. Then they would bring their cards to the party, and the guests would have to open the cards and figure out who they were from."

"Cool!" said Dawn. "They disguise their names."

"And we could call the party a Valentine Masquerade," added Kristy.

"The party guests will have to be old enough

to read," said Claudia thoughtfully. "Maybe the party should be for kids who are six and older."

"Oh, *please* make the cut-off age five," said Mallory, moaning. "If Claire is the only one in my family who can't come to the party, we will hear about it for the rest of our days."

"Who says your family is invited?" asked Kristy, but we knew she was teasing. Then she added, "Okay, the party will be for kids five and up."

"Great," the rest of us agreed.

The phone had rung then, so we weren't able to discuss party plans any further, but that was all right. We figured deciding on the theme was the hardest part of party planning, and that other things — games and refreshments — would be easy to plan later on. The only thing we needed to do right away (or at least soon) was send out invitations.

"I'll take care of that," said Claudia. "I'll draw something really cute. Then I'll ask Mom to copy it on the machine at the library." (Mrs. Kishi is the head librarian at our public library.)

However, by Saturday, Claud had not gotten around to the invitations, although she kept saying she was going to. Personally, I think this was for the best. Now don't get me wrong. Claud is one of my best friends and I

27

love her. But she is a horrible speller. If Claud had made the invitations, they probably would have read: ITS A HALIDAY! COME CELABRAT VANENTINS DAY WITH THE BSC. Or something like that.

The point is that when I showed up at the Pikes' on Saturday to baby-sit with Mallory, there were still no invitations for our party. (Oh, in case you're wondering, my friends and I usually do not baby-sit in pairs, but Mr. and Mrs. Pike insist on hiring two sitters when they need someone to watch over all seven of their younger kids. Mallory and I would be in charge that Saturday afternoon.)

All morning, rain had fallen. And it showed no sign of letting up. "The kids are going to be wired," I said to my mother, as I headed out our back door. "They've probably been cooped up for hours."

Mom smiled at me. "You'll think of something," she said brightly. (My mother is the reason I do not have much of a self-confidence problem.)

"Thanks," I said. "See you at dinnertime!"

I dashed across our yard. My house sits directly behind Mallory's. Our back windows face each other, and our yards meet just beyond one of the Pikes' flower beds.

Holding my umbrella low, I made a beeline

for the Pike patio and let myself in the door of the rec room.

"Hello?" I called.

"Stacey?" replied Mallory. She was upstairs somewhere. She ran down to me.

"Where is everyone?" I asked.

"Mom and Dad are in the living room. They're getting ready to leave."

"But where are the kids?"

"You don't want to know."

"I don't?" Uh-oh. "The house is awfully quiet," I said tentatively.

Mallory nodded. "The kids are upstairs in the bathroom. They're doing water experiments in the tub. Well, except for Nicky."

"Do they have permission?"

"Yes. Unfortunately."

"Where's Nicky?"

"Around somewhere. He's been sort of quiet today."

Hmm.

A few minutes later, Mr. and Mrs. Pike left. Mallory and I ventured upstairs and peeked in the bathroom. The tub was full of water, homemade boats, and sponges, but the kids were just sitting around. They looked as if they were out of ideas. Maybe they would let me empty the tub.

They did. While the water was gurgling

down the drain, Mallory said, "So. What are you guys going to do this afternoon?"

The reply was six sets of shoulders shrugging.

"It's too bad it isn't closer to Valentine's Day," said Mal. "You could start making your cards."

"Well," said Vanessa, "maybe we could get a head start."

"Wait, I've got a better idea!" I exclaimed. "How would you guys like to make the invitations for the Valentine Masquerade?"

"For your party?" said Margo.

Mallory brightened. "Sure!" she said. "We have construction paper and glue and stuff. You guys make the cards, and Stacey and I will write the party information on them. How does that sound?"

Mal received a variety of replies, ranging from "Very fun!" (Claire) to "Gnarly, man!" (Adam, who was kidding). However, Nicky, who had wandered into the bathroom, said nothing.

So Mal and I covered the kitchen table with newspapers, put out supplies, and let the kids go to it. We were busily giving out directions when, for some reason, I decided to take a head count.

Someone was missing.

"Where's Nicky?" I asked Mal.

"I don't know. Is he gone already? He's been *so* weird today."

"I'll go find him," I said. I checked the rec room and the bathroom. No Nicky. So I approached the boys' bedroom. The door was closed.

I knocked. "Nicky?" I called. "It's me, Stacey."

"Don't come in!" he shouted.

"Why not? What are you doing?"

"Nothing."

"Well, let me see. Can I *please* come in?"

"No, I'm busy."

"Hey, Nicky. What's the matter? Are you in trouble?"

"No."

"Nicky, I'm getting worried. Do I need to call your parents?"

"No!" This time his "no" sounded slightly frantic. "Don't call them!"

"Then let me — " (Suddenly the door flew open.) " — come in," I finished. I stepped into the room. "What are you doing in here by yourself?"

"You have to promise you won't tell," Nicky answered, closing the door.

"Okay . . . I won't tell."

Nicky pointed to an elaborate but half-finished valentine on his desk. He had obviously been working diligently on it.

"That's beautiful!" I exclaimed softly. "Who's it for?"

"It's for my, um, secret friend."

"Your secret friend?"

Nicky nodded. "She's a girl. She's younger than me. She's only in second grade."

"What's her name?" I asked.

"I'm not telling!" Nicky cried impatiently. "And don't *you* tell *any*one about this. I don't want my brothers to find out. They would never stop teasing me if they did."

"Okay. I said I'd keep your secret and I meant it. I'll leave now. I bet if you work really hard, you can finish the card before your brothers come back upstairs."

Nicky breathed a sigh of relief. "Thanks, Stacey," he said.

"You're welcome."

I left the room smiling. Nicky had a crush on a girl!

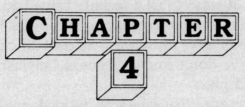

CHAPTER 4

I stood in the middle of my bedroom and turned around in a slow circle, taking in every inch of the room as I did so. Everything had to be perfect for Laine, who was arriving . . . today. Out of the corner of my eye I caught sight of Lennie, this rag doll that belongs to Claudia. Claud had brought Lennie over once for a slumber party and had forgotten to take her home. I grabbed Lennie and stuck her under my bed, decided that wasn't a very good hiding place, buried her under some clothes on the floor of the closet, thought again, and finally stuffed her into the clothes hamper and covered her with some underwear. That should hide her.

I checked over my room again. The poster of the kitten in the teacup (given to me by Mary Anne) had been taken off my wall. In its place, I had tacked up several photos of Retro, this singing group Laine likes. I had hidden my stuffed pig. In fact, I had hidden my entire pig collection. I just love pigs. Laine used to think that was funny. But I had a feeling she was way beyond pigs now. Actually, it wasn't just a feeling. Laine had said, during one of our recent phone conversations, "You still have those pigs, Stace?" (She'd giggled.) "I don't know. I guess I'm just way beyond pigs."

After one final check, I decided my room looked suitably adult. I dashed downstairs and opened the refrigerator. "Yikes! Mom, did you get the seltzer?" I asked. "Laine drinks seltzer now. She doesn't drink soda anymore, and I don't want — "

"Honey, the seltzer's in the cabinet near the sink. Put a bottle in the fridge so it can chill. And would you please calm down?"

I couldn't. I couldn't calm down. I raced around our house. It had to look perfect for Laine, just like my room did. I got rid of a couple of magazines that didn't seem sophisticated enough, then moved a copy of The New Yorker to the top of the stack. I put away my baby pictures and the pictures of my BSC friends and me on our trip to Disney World. I put away a couple of knickknacks that I knew Laine would think were tacky. She never used to think they were tacky, but that was a year ago, before she'd grown up so much.

34

By late in the morning I had begun another project. I was getting ready for a sleepover. The members of the BSC were going to spend the night at my house to welcome Laine to Stoneybrook. We planned to do the usual things — listen to music, experiment with our makeup and hair, and eat. Of course, the sleepover also had to be perfect. I pored over my collection of tapes, put away the children's music that I sometimes take along on baby-sitting jobs, and moved the newest, coolest tapes to the front of the case, where Laine would see them first. Once again, I despaired over the contents of the refrigerator, but then I decided my makeup collection was decent enough, so I felt better.

Early in the afternoon, Mom said, "Stacey, we should leave for the station now. Laine's train will be coming in soon."

"Just a minute!" I yelled from my room. Now I was making sure *I* looked perfect. I examined myself critically in the full-length mirror. This was the outfit I had chosen in which to meet Laine: a purple shirtwaist top over flowered leggings, my cowboy boots (cowgirl boots? cow*woman* boots?), a purple hair ornament made from shoelaces, and long dangly silver earrings. I passed my test.

Mom and I set out for the Stoneybrook station. We arrived five minutes before Laine's train did. When I saw its headlights shining down the tracks I murmured, "Here she comes." (I meant Laine, not the train.) I could feel my stomach turn to butterflies.

The train screeched its way into the station, eased to a stop, and opened its doors. I saw Laine the second she stepped onto the platform. She was hard to miss, considering she was wearing a jean *coat* with a *fur* collar (I sincerely hoped the fur was fake), black capri pants edged with lace, very chic black ankle boots, and on her head, a brilliant red over-sized beret.

Immediately, I felt slightly dorky. Even so, I called out, "Laine! Laine!" Mom and I waved frantically.

Laine nodded to us. "Hi!" she replied. She made her way to me, lugging along a stuffed duffel bag.

I ran toward her (a little too fast).

I crashed into her.

"Hey!" exclaimed Laine.

"Sorry," I said, giggling.

Laine didn't giggle. She greeted my mother. Then she set her bag on the platform and looked up and down the tracks. There wasn't much to see except the ticket window and a lot of trees. (Personally, I have grown to like the scenery.)

"Is this Stoneybrook?" Laine asked incredulously.

"The outskirts," I answered. "We'll drive you through town on our way home. Oh, Laine, I'm *so* glad to see you! I'm glad you decided to visit."

"Thanks," said Laine, smiling finally. "Me, too. Thank you for inviting me. Thank you, Mrs. McGill."

"We're going to have a party tonight," I told Laine. "My BSC friends are coming. Everyone wants to see you."

"A party? Great!"

Mom gave Laine a brief tour of Stoneybrook as she drove back to our house.

"Where's the town?" asked Laine.

My mouth dropped open. If Laine hadn't been thirteen years old, I might have thought she was becoming senile. "We just drove through it," I said.

"Through it?" Laine repeated. "Through the *town*? How did I miss it?"

"I don't know," I answered honestly. "I pointed out the pizza place and the library and those stores."

"But where's everything else?"

"There *is* nothing else."

"Gosh, what do people do for entertainment?"

"They go to New York," I said.

I felt better when we reached my house, though. Laine and I holed up in my room, lolled around on the floor, and talked the way we used to. Laine told me about King, who sounded . . . interesting.

"What do your parents think of his hair?" I asked. King's hair is purple, but only at the ends. Otherwise it's black, the way it's supposed to be. Every day he uses mousse and stuff to make it look bushy and spiky. (Most people can get their hair to look like that just by sleeping on it wet.)

Laine was carrying four pictures of King in her wallet. As she put them back, she shrugged. "I guess they like it okay. No, that's not true. They hate it. But they stopped mentioning that to me. . . . Do you have a boyfriend yet?"

"Laine!" I exclaimed. "Don't you think I would have told you if I did?"

Laine smiled. "I guess so. What about that guy who took you to the winter dance? Do you like him?"

"Austin? No. I mean, I do like him, but we're just friends."

"Oh. Don't you *want* a boyfriend?"

"Sure. But he has to be the right guy. I don't want to spend a lot of time hanging around someone I don't like. What's the point in that?"

"I like King!" Laine exclaimed.

"I didn't say you didn't. Sheesh."

"Okay, okay."

My BSC friends started to show up around suppertime. Even though there were eight of us, I had ordered only one hoagie (vegetarian, so Dawn would eat it) because we always end up pigging out on pretzels and chips and nuts and stuff.

When we had downed the hoagie we went upstairs and jammed ourselves into my room, along with the overnight packs, sleeping bags, bowls of junk food, cans of soda, and a bottle of seltzer for Laine. I turned on the tape deck. Claud and I sat on the stool in front of my dressing table. Claud started to paint her nails. Jessi began playing with Dawn's long hair. In a matter of minutes, everyone was experimenting with makeup, hair, and nails. Except for Laine. She sat on the bed, her legs crossed, and leafed through a magazine.

"You know who's cute?" said Claud, carefully painting a gold dot onto a bright red fingernail. "Ron Belkis," she answered herself. "Too bad he's in seventh grade. All the cute guys are the wrong age."

"You could go out with a seventh-grader, Claud," said Dawn. "That would be okay. You know who *I* think is cute? Dave Griffin."

"How old is he?" asked Laine.

"Our age. He's in eighth grade."

Laine nodded. "But even thirteen-year-old boys are pretty dorky," she said.

I watched Mary Anne get all huffy. "Not *all* thirteen-year-old boys. Logan isn't dorky!" she cried.

"Neither is Bart," said Kristy.

"Sorry," said Laine. "It's just that King is . . . well, he's fifteen."

"Can he drive?" asked Kristy.

"No."

"Vote?"

"Of course not!"

"Then what's the point in — "

I interrupted Kristy. I cut her off mid-sentence, before a fight could break out. "Laine, you know what? You're going to be here for our Valentine Dance," I said. "Wouldn't it be neat if you could go to it? *We're* all going. Most of us are going with the same guys who took us to the Winter Wonderland Dance."

"Not me," spoke up Dawn. "I don't think I'll ever go anywhere with Price again. We don't have a thing in common."

"Price," repeated Laine. "Awesome name."

"Boring dude," said Dawn. She was hiding a smile.

"Dude?" Laine said. "Sheesh. That word went out with the sixties."

"The sixties are back," snapped Claud.

Yikes. What was wrong with everyone?

My friends were quiet for a moment. Then Laine yawned, stretched, and said, "So what are we going to do tonight?"

I sneaked a glance at Claud. Maybe Laine was senile after all. Then I said. "We're — we're having a sleepover, remember?"

"Of course I remember. But what are we going to *do?*"

"Eat," answered Claud.

"I'm on a diet," said Laine.

"Gab," suggested Jessi.

"Gossip," added Mal.

"Beautify ourselves," said Kristy, trying not to laugh.

Since none of these answers seemed to impress Laine, I spoke up, sounding falsely bright. "We're going to find you a date for the dance."

"*When* is this dance?"

"Friday night."

"Six days away," added Mary Anne. "Six long days."

"I don't know . . ." Laine's voice trailed off.

"What do you mean?" I said. "What will

41

you do Friday night if you don't go? The rest of us will be at the dance."

"Well, what would you be doing if you weren't going to the dance?" asked Laine.

There was a pause. "Homework?" suggested Mal.

"On *Friday night?*"

I sighed impatiently. "So go to the dance."

"I'll have to check with King," Laine answered.

I saw Dawn roll her eyes.

"Hey, you know what?" exclaimed Claud, who had finished painting her nails and was now leafing gingerly through the *TV Guide.* "*To Kill a Mockingbird* is on!"

"All *right!*" cried Laine. She sounded genuinely excited.

We tuned into the movie. Everyone had fun that night. Even Laine.

CHAPTER 5

Mondy

Marlyn and Carolin arnold are much more fun to babysit now that their not look the same any more. Its so nice to be abel to tell them a part. They are two very diferent kids even if they are twines. Today they mad valentimes for the party. They worked hard but they had fun. And Carlin has a secret she likes a certain boy but she wont say what is his name.

Marilyn and Carolyn Arnold are identical twins, but you would hardly know it. They used to look and dress *exactly* the same. (This was not their idea; it was their parents' idea. Their mom and dad would make them wear identical outfits, right down to the jewelry!) But the girls were not happy that way. They knew that under their skin they were different people. So how come they had to look alike?

They didn't. Just after their eighth birthday, the girls were finally able to talk to their mom and tell her how they felt. Now, the girls wear their hair differently, and each dresses in her own style. Marilyn wears her hair long and dresses in simple, classic clothes. She likes wool kilts, plaid dresses, jean skirts, and pretty shirts. Carolyn, who's more outgoing than her twin, cut her hair short, leaving longer curls down her back. She likes trendier clothes — leggings, oversized sweaters, short skirts. However, Marilyn is the decision-maker. She tends to be the leader, and Carolyn the follower. Also, Marilyn's main interest is playing the piano, while Carolyn likes (loves) science. Now, the girls are twin second-graders whom the teachers and kids at Stoneybrook Elementary can finally tell apart.

Their baby-sitters can tell them apart, too.

But you know what? When the members of the BSC first sat for the twins, the only way we could tell Marilyn from Carolyn was by looking at their wrists and reading the name bracelets their mom had bought for them. Boy, was that a drag. No wonder the twins were unhappy. How would you feel if your friends didn't know who you were unless they read a sign? (You'd probably feel as though you had no identity.)

But that's in the past. And I was glad. My friends and I look forward to sitting for Marilyn and Carolyn, knowing they can't mix us up anymore, and they won't be terrors.

It was Monday, two days after Laine had come to Stoneybrook. Claud was sitting for the twins from three-thirty until five-fifteen (just before our club meeting). The day was sunny and the air felt springlike, considering that it was only early February, and that the groundhog, Saugatuck Sam, had seen his shadow, so we were supposed to be having six more weeks of winter. (*Now* I was worried about global warming.)

"Do you guys want to play outside today?" Claudia asked the twins after Mrs. Arnold had left.

"Yes!" cried Carolyn, but Marilyn nudged her. "I mean no," Carolyn corrected herself.

"Marilyn and I want you to help us make valentines for the Masquerade, now that we know who to make them for."

The Pike kids' invitations had been sent out and everyone had replied.

We'd invited about twenty-two kids, and fifteen were going to be able to come to the party. This was our guest list: Margo, Nicky, Claire, and Vanessa Pike (the triplets had decided they were too old for Valentine's Day parties); Matt and Haley Braddock; James and Mathew Hobart; Becca Ramsey; Charlotte Johanssen; Buddy Barrett; Karen Brewer; David Michael Thomas; and the twins.

We gave a list to each guest so he or she could make cards for the other guests. Or buy them, of course, but we figured making cards was more fun, and that most kids would want to do that.

No wonder the twins were eager for Claud to help them. Claud is so artistic and creative. And sure enough, when Marilyn said, "We want to make really *special* valentines, Claudia. Not just regular old hearts with poems," Claud replied, "How about 3-D cards? You know, pop-ups?"

The twins loved the idea, so Claud helped them find some art supplies and set up a work space in their rec room. "Now, 3-D is really easy," she said, when she and the girls were seated at the table. "All you do is take a strip of paper and fold it back and forth, back and forth, back and forth, like an accordian." Claudia demonstrated. This is how her folded paper looked:

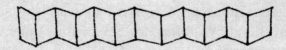

"Then," she continued, "glue one end to your card. On the other end, glue whatever it is that you want to pop up. Like this little heart. See?"

Claud opened and closed her card. Each time she opened it, the heart jumped out. The paper worked like a spring.

"Cool!" exclaimed the girls.

"I'm going to make a *huge* jumping heart for — " Carolyn started to say. "For — for, um . . ."

"Yes?" teased Marilyn.

"For you-know-who." Carolyn began to cut a giant heart out of a piece of pink construction paper.

"You-know-who is the boy she likes," Marilyn informed Claud.

"Oh! You — " (Claud almost said, "You have a crush on a boy?" but she decided that might embarrass Carolyn.) Instead she said, "Is this boy going to be at the Valentine Masquerade?"

"Yup," replied Carolyn. She glued red glitter to the heart. "And you know what? He's an *older* boy."

Claud didn't panic. When you're in second grade, an older boy could be a third-grader, which was nothing to worry about.

"Yeah," said Marilyn, "he's in third grade," (Aha! thought Claud), "but Carolyn won't tell me who he is. I know he'll be at the party, though."

"Well, you won't tell me the name of the boy *you* like," said Carolyn to Marilyn. "And I know you like someone."

"I guess," answered Marilyn, blushing. "But I'm not going to make a big goopy card for him. Just a regular one."

The twins worked busily.

"How are you going to sign your cards?" Claud asked after awhile.

Marilyn answered immediately. "I'm going

to sign some of mine by drawing a picture of a horse. Get it?" she said.

Carolyn and Claudia frowned.

"The horse will be a *mare*. Mare for Marilyn!" said Marilyn.

"Neat," said Carolyn. "I might sign some of mine with a number code. I'll number each letter in my name. Like, A would be one, B would be two." She began scribbling the code on a piece of paper. "So C-A-R-O-L-Y-N would be three, one, eighteen, fifteen, twelve, twenty-five, fourteen. Do you think anyone will figure out that code?"

"I don't know," answered Claud. "It's a good one."

"Oh, this party is going to be so, so fun!" exclaimed Carolyn. She sat back. "I wonder if my valentine is big enough."

"If it were any bigger," said Claud, "you'd have to take it to the party in a truck."

Carolyn nodded, satisfied. "Good," she said. "Then you-know-who will like his card."

Claud smiled. She had forgotten how much fun Valentine's Day secrets could be.

CHAPTER 6

"Laine. Hey, Laine! Wake up . . . come on. It's time to get going." I was leaning into our guest room, whispering to Laine, who was a lump in the bed.

After a moment, she groaned. Then she said slowly, "I cannot believe I am on vacation and I'm going to *school* today."

I paused. "Well, you don't have to come. You can stay home again."

"That's okay." Laine buried her head under the pillow and murmured, "I'll come. I'll come. And don't worry. I won't make you late."

Laine had entertained herself the day before while I was in school. I was pretty sure she had been bored out of her mind. The first thing she said to me when I walked through the door that afternoon was, "Thank goodness you have a television!" She had watched something like five straight hours of TV. So I took her downtown for awhile. It was when we were sitting in Renwick's, sharing French fries (Laine ate about three) and drinking seltzer, that I sprung my news on her.

"Guess what," I said. "I got permission for you to come to school with me tomorrow. You won't have to spend the day alone."

"Come to your school?" repeated Laine.

"Yeah. You can follow me around, go to my classes."

"But, Anastasia, I'm on vacation. The idea is *not* to be in school."

More and more, Laine was calling me Anastasia. And I did not like it. Mostly, people call me by my full name when they're angry at me. Or frustrated with me. I knew Laine used the name just because it sounded more grown-up. Still, every time I heard it, it took me by surprise. I felt like snapping, "What did I do?"

"You don't *have* to come to school," I replied. "It was just an idea. I want you to meet my friends. I mean, the ones who aren't in the BSC. I want you to see SMS. I don't know. It's like . . . we used to be part of each other's lives. When I was living in New York and we went to the same school, we were practically sharing one life. Now our lives are so different. We talk a lot, but we hardly see each other. I feel as if I'm losing half of *me*, and I'm trying to figure out how to get myself back. I miss you, Laine, I really do."

Laine smiled. "I'd like to come to school with you tomorrow," she said.

Which was why I was leaning into the guest room on Tuesday morning, trying to rouse her.

"How are you getting to school today?" Laine mumbled from under her pillow.

"Walking," I replied. "Mom drives me if it rains, but the weather is supposed to be gorgeous again today. Early spring. Saugatuck Sam must have had an off day when he peeked out of his hole."

Laine giggled. She tossed her pillow away, flung back the covers, and sat up. "You're demented!" she cried.

"Thank you. I take that as a compliment."

Silly me. I also took it as a sign that the day would go well.

Laine and Mom and I ate a quick breakfast. As we were finishing, I said, "Hey, Laine. Remember that telephone code we used to have?"

"The school code?" asked Laine.

I nodded. In New York, Laine and I had gone to the same school but had lived in different apartment buildings. If one of us wanted to meet the other before school, we would call, let the phone ring once, and hang up. (There was no reason we couldn't have made an actual phone call; we just liked the idea of using a code.)

"Well, Mallory Pike and I have a code now," I said. "Look out the window." I pointed out our kitchen window to the back of the Pikes' house. "See that white towel on Mal's patio?"

"Yeah?" said Laine.

"That means Mal wants to walk to school with Mary Anne and Dawn and me. A red towel means she has to walk her brothers and sisters to school."

Laine gave me a funny look. "Why don't you guys just call each other?" she suggested, frowning.

I shrugged. I could feel my face reddening. "I don't know," I replied. "How come you and I didn't just call each other?"

"Because we were only ten," said Laine.

Mom put an end to the conversation. "You better get a move on, honey," she said to me. "It's getting late."

"Yikes, you're right!" I exclaimed. "And there's Mal!" (She was standing on the patio, peering at our house.)

Laine and I left in a frantic hurry. We ran to Mal's, and the three of us ran to Mary Anne and Dawn's. Then the *five* of us ran to SMS, picking up other friends along the way.

I was in a good mood by the time we reached school.

Apparently, Laine wasn't.

Here are a few of the things that happened that day:

Laine and I ditched a study hall and joined Claud and Mary Anne, who were working in the library. As the four of us sat at a table, Laine gazed outside and said, "How long is this period?"

"Exactly forty-two minutes," Claud answered.

"Enough time to run downtown and go to the coffee shop?"

"Well, yes," I said. "If we could leave school."

"You can't leave school?"

"Nope." I shook my head.

Mary Anne looked surprised. "We can't leave campus during school hours," she said. (Frankly, I don't think the idea had ever occurred to her.) "Not without an adult. You know, like on a field trip."

Laine rolled her eyes.

"Well, we *can't*," I said defensively. "It's hard enough to cut study hall. I don't particularly want to be suspended."

(At this point, I waited for a response from Laine but got none.)

Later, during a class, Laine was amazed that

only one student at a time was allowed to use the bathroom.

"What a stupid rule," she whispered to me.

"It's so kids can't duck out of class together and fool around."

"Well, what if two kids both need to use the bathroom *really* badly?"

"I don't know," I replied crankily. "I guess the teacher would make an exception. And keep your voice down, Laine. We aren't supposed to be talking."

Laine rolled her eyes.

I thought lunch might come as a relief to Laine. We have practically no cafeteria rules (except the obvious ones, like don't throw food). "See?" I said, as we entered the cafeteria. "We can sit wherever we want, with whomever we want. We can eat whatever we want. We can change places. We can go back and buy more food."

I had even arranged to sit with some boys. Usually Claud, Dawn, Mary Anne, Kristy, and I and *sometimes* Logan sit together, but I thought Laine might be tired of seeing nothing but the faces of BSC members, so I asked a bunch of other kids to join us. Among them were Pete Black, Rick Chow, and Austin Bentley.

"Hey, lookit this," said Austin, halfway through lunch period. "If you poke pretzel sticks into a prune it sort of looks like a space satellite."

We laughed — except for Laine, who looked dumbfounded, and except for Pete, who couldn't take his eyes off Laine. Oh, and also except for Kristy, who had been glowering silently throughout lunch.

Mary Anne nudged Kristy. "What's wrong?" she asked.

"Bart might not be able to go to the dance on Friday," she said crisply, biting off each word. "He calls me at home this morning and has the nerve to tell me he might want to watch a game on TV then." She shifted her gaze to Pete. "What are *you* staring at?" she demanded.

Pete was still watching Laine. He didn't even hear Kristy.

"Jerk," Kristy muttered. I wasn't sure if she meant Pete or Bart.

"Hey!" exclaimed Rick, getting into the spirit of the prune sculptures. "If you take a *bunch* of prunes and join them with pretzel sticks, you can build molecules." He held up a sculpture. "This is water," he announced. "H-two-oh. And this one is carbon monoxide."

"Thank you, Professor Chow," I said, giggling.

"Where does he get the *nerve*?" sputtered Kristy.

Dawn nudged her. "Give it a rest," she whispered.

"Boys are pains," grumbled Kristy, but then she did keep quiet.

Which was a good thing, because Laine was giving her a strange look.

Lunch continued. The boys built prune models of hydrogen peroxide and some sulphur stuff.

While Rick was trying to figure out how to make triethanolomine (or something like that), a silence fell over our table. And Pete chose that moment to murmur to Laine, "You have hair like gossamer."

Finally Laine laughed. It was the only time she laughed while she was at my school.

CHAPTER 7

That evening I had to do homework. I was sorry not to spend all my time with Laine, but homework was homework. However, near nine o'clock I decided I needed a break, so I joined Laine in the guest room, where she was reading a book.

"You know, Pete Black likes you," I said to her. I curled up in the armchair while Laine stuck a marker in her book, then rolled onto her side and propped up her head with her hand.

"He wasn't very subtle," she agreed.

"I wonder where he ever found the word *gossamer*."

"Who knows? It sounds like it belongs on a vocabulary list for a fairy-tale book. Along with *swoon* and *parapet*."

"And *swanlike neck*," I added.

"I'm surprised he didn't tell me I have ruby-red lips."

"Give him a chance," I said. And then another wonderful thought sprang into my mind. "Hey! Invite him to the Valentine Dance!" I cried. "You know he'd go with you. And then you'd have a date on Friday."

"But Anastasia, he is *such* a dweeb."

"Pete?" I said. "Oh, Laine. No, he isn't. Not really. You don't know him the way we do. He's smart and funny — "

"He told me I have hair like gossamer."

"I think that's sort of sweet. Don't you?"

Laine shrugged. "King would never say something like that."

"What *would* he say?" I asked. "I mean, how would he compliment you?"

Again, Laine shrugged. Then she looked thoughtful. At last she said, "He'd say to me, 'Awesome, Babe.' That's what he calls me. *Babe.*"

"He calls you *Babe?*" I was incredulous. No one had ever called me *Babe.* And I didn't think I wanted anyone to. Unless maybe some incredible performer was singing a song just for me. He could call me *Babe* in the song. That would be the only exception to the Babe Rule.

Laine was smiling. "Yup," she replied. "King calls me Babe and I call him Heart. Like in the King of Hearts. The King of *my* Heart."

I nodded. "Well, anyway," I went on, "the King of your Heart is back in New York. And I'm sure Pete Black wants to take you to the Valentine Dance. You do want to go to the dance, don't you?"

"Yes," Laine answered.

"So what's the big deal? Go with Pete."

"The big deal is that Pete Black is a dweeb. Like I said."

"No, he isn't. But if he was, why should you care? You'll go to the dance with him on Friday. Then on Saturday you'll go back to New York and King. It's not like Pete will ask you to go steady."

"But what will people think?"

"What people?" I asked, confused.

Laine threw me a look that plainly said, "What are you? Crazy?" She spoke slowly when she answered me, as if I might not be able to keep up with her words if she spoke more quickly. "Everyone . . . at . . . the . . . dance . . . Your friends . . . The other kids . . . The teachers."

"They don't know you," I replied. "They'll just think they see Pete, who's a nice kid, dancing with some strange girl."

"Thanks a lot!" cried Laine.

"Oh, come on. You know what I mean. Not

that you're strange. That you're a stranger."

"I'm not a stranger to the other members of the BSC."

"And neither is Pete," I pointed out.

Laine grew silent. She examined her sweater and removed two tiny pieces of lint from it. I thought I saw her mouth tremble.

"Laine, what's the real problem?" I asked.

"I guess I'm afraid of what *King* will think."

"What do you mean?" I asked.

"If I'm being, you know, unfaithful to him."

"But this wouldn't be unfaithful. The dance wouldn't mean anything. Think of Pete more as your escort than as your date."

Laine squirmed. "I don't know . . ."

"Oh, go on. Call him," I urged her.

More squirming. Laine brushed back her hair.

"You aren't *afraid* to call him, are you?"

"Of course not," replied Laine. "Watch this."

Laine stood up. She led me into Mom's room. She reached for the phone on the night table. And the phone rang!

"Yiiiiiii!" we shrieked.

I composed myself. I answered the phone.

"Hello?" said an unfamiliar voice.

"Hello?" I replied.

"Um, hi. This is King. How's Ba — I mean how is it there in the sticks?"

"Fine," I answered tightly. I motioned to Laine. "It's King," I mouthed.

Laine grabbed the receiver. "Hi!" she cried. "Hi, Heart. It's me, Babe."

I sat on the edge of Mom's bed, next to Laine. I planned to give her moral support in case she had a difficult time telling King about Pete. But after several seconds had passed silently, I glanced at her and found her staring openly at me. She cocked her head toward the door.

"What?" I whispered.

Laine nodded to the door a few more times. So I looked at the door.

Exasperated, Laine covered the mouthpiece with her hand. Then she whispered loudly, "I need some privacy."

"Oh!" I exclaimed, jumping to my feet. "Sorry." I left Laine in a hurry and retreated to my room. I picked up a pencil and tried to concentrate on my homework. But bits of Laine's conversation with King kept floating down the hall and into my ears.

". . . to a Valentine's Day dance!" I heard her say, and giggle. There was silence. Then, "Yeah. I know. . . . I know." A minute later, I thought I caught the word "childish." Laine must be telling King about some of the children my friends and I baby-sit for, I thought. I smiled, glad to have Laine part of my life here in Stoneybrook.

Fifteen minutes later, Laine had hung up the phone and sauntered into my room. Before she had a chance to sit down, though, the phone rang again. I dashed back to Mom's room, calling, "I'll get it!" I picked up the phone, mid-ring. "Hello?"

"Hi, Stacey?" (Another male voice, vaguely familiar.)

"Yeah?"

"Oh, hi, this is Pete. Um, Pete Black."

"Hey!" I cried. "What's up?"

"Well, I was just wondering. Is Laine there? Could I talk to her?"

"Sure!" I exclaimed. This was great! I was sure Pete wanted to invite Laine to the dance. I was so proud of him. Plus, now Laine really would have a date for Friday night, so she could come to the dance with the rest of the BSC and *our* dates. What a perfect way to finish up Laine's first visit to Stoneybrook.

I called Laine to the phone, whispered who was on the other end, and then edged toward the doorway. But Laine reached out and caught at the sleeve of my shirt, asking me to stay.

So I did, not sure why she wanted me around for this conversation. Especially when

Laine's end of it consisted of her saying, "Yeah . . . yeah," about fifteen times. And finishing up with, "Okay. Thanks. I'll see you Friday. . . . Yeah. . . . 'Bye."

When Laine hung up the receiver, she fell onto Mom's bed and giggled uncontrollably. She laughed so hard she cried.

"What?" I asked. "Did Pete ask you to the dance?"

"Yes!" exclaimed Laine. Finally she calmed down enough to say, "Pete told me he thinks I'm cute. And that my eyes are like limpid pools. We have to add *limpid* to our vocabulary list, Anastasia." Laine was overcome by giggles again. But she managed to say with a gasp, "Oh! I *have* to call King to tell him this." Then she stared at me.

I took that as my cue to leave.

I didn't return to my room, though. Instead, I hovered in the hall, shamelessly listening to Laine's conversation. For someone who had been so reluctant to talk about something, she didn't seem to have any trouble letting King know that she now was, in fact, going to a dance with another boy. She told him all about her very brief encounters with Pete that day — and she made Pete sound like a fool.

I wandered back to my room. Something was wrong. Did Laine have to act this way to make sure King wouldn't feel threatened by

Pete? Well, that wasn't fair. Not to Pete and not to King. Not to Laine, either. I found myself growing angry. But, I reminded myself, Laine and I have been mad at each other before. We've had some *huge* fights. And we've always made up.

CHAPTER 8

Wednesday

There's Valentine fever at the Hobart house! Today I sat for Mathew, James, and Johnny, while Ben went to the library with Mallory. Mathew and James are going to the Masquerade, and they are so excited. They've never been to a Valentine's Day party. It will be a big deal for them. Guess what. I left my job early -- because Ben came home early. He and Mal had *an argument at the library, and Ben stormed home....*

My friends and I like the Hobarts very much. As I said, the Hobarts live across the street from Claud, in Mary Anne's old house. They bought it when her dad got remarried and the Spiers moved to Dawn's house.

There are four Hobart boys. Ben, as I've mentioned, is eleven and is sort of Mal's boyfriend. They go to the movies a lot and study together at the library. Then there's James, who's eight; Mathew, who's six; and Johnny, who's four. The Hobarts moved here from *Australia*. (And I thought Dawn had come a long distance when she moved from California.) When the Hobarts first came to this country, they spoke with these wonderful accents, but already the boys' accents are beginning to fade. The Hobarts are making friends in the neighborhood, and we sit for them pretty often, so we invited James and Mathew to the Masquerade. (Ben's too old and Johnny's too young. Ben promised Johnny a special treat on Saturday so that he wouldn't feel left out of the celebrations.)

When Jessi arrived at the Hobarts' on Wednesday afternoon, she found three exuberant little boys. They were excited about Valentine's Day, and James and Mathew were looking forward to the party. Jessi thought they might be looking forward to it a bit too much.

"We've never been to a party celebrating Valentine's Day," said James to Jessi. He took a bite out of a pear, then wiped his chin with a napkin.

Jessi was sitting at the Hobarts' kitchen table while she and the boys shared an after-school snack from the fruit bowl. "I think you'll have fun," Jessi replied. "You'll know the other kids at the party. You'll get tons of valentines. Maybe you'll win a prize, playing a game."

"Awesome," James said.

"Yeah, awesome," added Mathew. "Jessi? What do you wear to a Valentine masquerade?"

"I'm going to wear — " Jessi began to say.

But Mathew interrupted her. "No, I mean, what do six-year-old boys wear to a Valentine masquerade?"

"And eight-year-old boys?" asked James.

"Oh," said Jessi. "Well, you can wear — "

But again Mathew cut her off. "I'll *show* you what I want to wear! I hope it's all right."

"Yeah, I'll show you, too!" cried James.

They abandoned their fruit and ran out of the kitchen, knocking each other into the doorway as they squeezed through it. Moments later, they thundered down the stairs and reappeared in the kitchen.

"Look!" they exclaimed.

James held up two coat hangers, on which was displayed a handsome black suit. "I will wear my new necktie," he added.

Mathew also held up two hangers. On his was displayed a blue suit. "Mum said I may wear my good shoes," he told Jessi.

For a moment Jessi couldn't speak. How could she tell the boys that the Masquerade was not going to be so fancy? That the other guests would be wearing jeans and school clothes? That James and Mathew would be the only kids in suits?

"Those . . . your suits are wonderful," said Jessi at last. "But you know what? You're going to play games at the party. You'll be running around. So you might want to think about jeans or something."

"Jeans!" repeated James, horrified. "I can't wear a carnation with jeans. And I can't give flowers to my date if I'm wearing jeans."

"Date? What date?" asked Jessi. She and the boys had finished their snack, and Jessi was tidying up the kitchen. Johnny had settled down with some fat crayons and a stack of drawing paper. But Mathew and James were following Jessi around, wide-eyed.

"Our dates at the Valentine's Day party," replied James. He sounded exasperated, as if he had already told Jessi a million times about the dates.

Jessi put the sponge back in its holder. She eyed James and Mathew. "Who did you invite to the party?" she asked them.

James shrugged.

Mathew said, "We don't know yet. But we're going to invite them."

"Girls?" Jessi said, just to make sure.

"Yes," replied James. "And like the men on the telly, we'll wear our best suits — "

" — with red carnation flowers," added Mathew.

"Yes, with red carnations. And we'll bring flowers for our dates."

"You guys," said Jessi, "maybe I should tell you what you're going to do at the party. You'll be playing games, like I said. And you'll be eating messy food — cupcakes with frosting, red punch, crumbly cookies, sticky candy."

"Oh," said James and Mathew.

"I think," Jessi continued, "that the other kids will be wearing play clothes. Or maybe school clothes. But they won't be very dressed up."

"Even the girls?" asked Mathew.

"Even the girls," replied Jessi.

The boys were quiet for a few moments, and Jessi thought she knew what they were thinking. When the Hobarts first moved here from Australia, some of the kids teased them because of their accents, or because the boys didn't understand certain American expressions or slang words. The Hobarts had worked hard to fit in with their neighbors and classmates. They wouldn't want to jeopardize their work by going to the Valentine Masquerade in suits and ties, bearing flowers.

"Also," said Jessi, "bringing flowers for your dates is a nice idea, but I don't think any of the other boys will be quite so thoughtful."

"Will they wear carnation flowers?" asked Mathew.

Jessi shook her head.

"Will they invite dates?" asked James, sounding as if he knew what Jessi's answer would be.

"No," said Jessi softly. The boys looked awfully disappointed. "Hey!" she exclaimed. "There is one thing you can do to get ready for the party."

"What is it?" Mathew wanted to know.

"Have you made your valentines yet?"

"Oh, we don't need to," said James. "Our mum found heaps of Valentine's Day cards in the stores."

"You bought your cards?"

71

"We're going to," Mathew answered.

"But *making* cards is much more fun," said Jessi. "You get paper and scissors and glue and markers. You cut out hearts. You draw pictures. You write funny messages. Johnny?" asked Jessi. (He glanced up from his drawing.) "You can make valentines, too."

The boys seemed intrigued by the idea and helped Jessi find art supplies. Jessi was covering the kitchen table with newspapers when she heard the Hobarts' front door open, then bang closed.

Her heart began to pound.

She mustered her courage and ran for the front hall. Halfway there, she bumped into someone tall.

She screamed.

"Jessi?"

The voice sounded familiar. Jessi realized she'd been squeezing her eyes shut. She opened them. Standing in front of her was Ben Hobart.

"Ben! You almost gave me a heart attack!" cried Jessi. "What are you doing home so early?"

Ben scowled. "Ask Mallory," he said crossly.

"Why?" ventured Jessi.

"Because she can explain why she's mad at

me. I can't. I don't even know what we were fighting about."

"Oh, no. You had a fight?"

"Yes. In the library. And the librarian threw us out. We might not even go to the dance on Friday."

"Well, I guess I'll leave," said Jessi quickly. "Your brothers are about to make valentines. The art supplies are on the counter in the kitchen. Um, your mom can pay me some other time. See ya!" Jessi left quickly.

She ran most of the way to her house and phoned Mal as soon as she'd taken off her jacket. "What happened?" were the first words out of her mouth. "You and Ben had a fight? I can't believe it."

"Believe it." Mal paused. Then she said, "How did you know we had a fight?"

"I was baby-sitting at the Hobarts'," Jessi replied. "I was there when Ben came home from the library."

"That's right. I forgot." Mal sighed. "It was such a *stupid* fight. We were looking up something in the card catalogue. I said to look according to subject, and Ben wanted to look up different authors. I said his way was slower, he said my way was slower, and before I knew it, this librarian was rushing across the room, going 'Shhh! SHHH!' Then she asked what was wrong, and when we tried to tell her, we began fighting all over again. So she said we would have to leave. When we got outside, I yelled to Ben, 'I hope you have fun at the dance, because *I'm* not going with you!' Then I came home."

"Oh, Mallory," said Jessi. "You know, I'm beginning to worry about the dance. I have a weird feeling about it. I don't think Laine really wants to go to it. Especially not with Pete Black. And Kristy and Bart are mad at each other, and now you and *Ben* are mad at each other." Jessi paused, then gasped.

"What's wrong?" asked Mal.

"You don't think these things are happening because the dance is going to be on Friday the thirteenth? Do you?"

Mal wasn't sure.

Neither was Jessi.

CHAPTER 9

"It's a bad omen," said Mallory ominously. "A very bad omen."

Laine rolled her eyes. But Mary Anne said, "I agree."

"It's not an omen," Kristy spoke up. "It's *boys*. They are only trouble."

"I'll say," said Mallory.

The Wednesday meeting of the BSC was not off to a good start. Half of my friends were in foul moods. Kristy was upset because of her argument with Bart. Mal was upset because of her fight with Ben. And now Mary Anne was angry with Logan. And the meeting hadn't officially started yet. The time was only 5:20. The gripe session could go on for another ten minutes before Kristy called the BSC members to order.

"Mary Anne?" I said. "What exactly did Logan do?" I wasn't sure I had the story straight yet.

"He talked to me about dancing on Friday."

I nodded. "Mm-hmm."

"*Dancing*," Mary Anne repeated.

"And?" said Laine.

"So I don't dance, remember?" Mary Anne seemed frustrated.

"What do you mean, you don't dance?" asked Laine.

"Just that. I never dance. Well, I *hardly* ever dance. I don't like to. And Logan knows it. Anyway, it didn't bother Logan before. He understands that I'm — you know — shy."

Laine frowned. "What *do* you and Logan do at dances?" she asked.

"Oh, eat. Walk around. Talk to people."

"Fascinating," said Laine, and Mary Anne blushed.

I decided I better rescue Mary Anne. "So today Logan was talking about dancing on Friday?"

Mary Anne nodded. Her eyes had filled with tears. She couldn't speak.

"Did you have a fight?" asked Dawn gently.

"Not exactly." Mary Anne's voice was wobbly. "I just sort of reminded him that *I* probably wouldn't be dancing with him. I said he could dance with you guys. And then he looked all disappointed."

"That's sweet!" exclaimed Claudia. "He just

wants to dance with you, Mary Anne. That's all."

"I know. But it led to this big discussion, and — "

"You're still going, aren't you? To the dance, I mean," said Jessi. "If *Mal* doesn't go and Kristy doesn't go — "

"Wait a second!" It was my turn to interrupt. "What's happening here? Are we all crazy? Maybe there's a full moon."

"It's because Friday the thirteenth is coming," said Mal. "Jessi and I figured it out yesterday."

I didn't believe *that*, but I was getting worried about the dance anyway. I was afraid my friends were going to ruin it with their silly fights. I knew Laine thought she was more mature than the members of the BSC, and I was afraid a fiasco at the dance would just prove it to her. So I certainly hoped Kristy, Mallory, and Mary Anne could pull themselves together by Friday evening.

"You know," Laine spoke up, "you guys are going to spoil the dance."

I was surprised to hear *Laine* say what *I'd* been thinking, but now maybe *I* wouldn't have to say anything.

"Oh, no one's going to spoil the dance," said Dawn.

"Someone might," Laine replied. "You're involved in such ridiculous fights. I can just imagine what will happen on Friday. Why don't you grow up and quit — "

"Five-thirty!" cried Kristy. "Time for our meeting. Order, order."

"You interrupted me," Laine said to Kristy.

"Fellow BSC members," Kristy continued, "you will note that a guest is attending today's meeting. Will the guest please be quiet?" (Laine clucked her tongue and looked annoyed. But she did keep quiet.) "Any club business?" asked Kristy.

"We should talk about the Valentine Masquerade," said Claud.

By then, I'd told Laine about our party, but she hadn't offered any opinions. I didn't know whether to feel relieved or worried by that.

"Mary Anne and I have been cleaning up the barn," said Dawn. (An old barn stands in the yard behind Dawn and Mary Anne's farmhouse. It isn't used for anything except storage.) "Having the party there is a great idea," she went on. "The barn's not heated, but it's warmer than being outside. Let's just hope for a sunny day. Anyway, if the kids make a mess in the barn, no one will care."

"Is the menu the same?" asked Kristy.

"Yup," replied Claud. "Cupcakes, candy hearts, cookies, and punch."

"Very well-balanced," commented Dawn, and we laughed.

"The kids are working on their valentines," reported Mal. "At least, my brothers and sisters are."

"So's Becca," said Jessi. "And Charlotte. And the Hobart boys."

"And Matt and Haley Braddock," added Mary Anne. "And Buddy and the twins. What about Karen and David Michael, Kristy?"

"Finished. They finished over the weekend. That's great, then. Each of the guests will be ready on Saturday. The party's going to be terrific!"

Ring, ring.

I dove for the phone. "Hello, Baby-sitters Club," I said. I listened for a moment. "Hi, Mr. Marshall. . . . A week from Monday? I'll call you right back. . . . Okay. . . . 'Bye." I hung up. "Mr. Marshall needs a sitter for Nina and Eleanor," I told my friends. "Monday evening. Seven to nine-thirty."

Mary Anne checked the calendar in the BSC record book. "Let's see. Stacey and Kristy, you're free."

"You take it, Stace," said Kristy. "You live closer to the Marshalls."

"Thanks!" I exclaimed. I called Mr. Marshall back to tell him I'd be sitting. As soon as I hung up, the phone rang again.

The meeting became quite busy.

But Laine looked bored. Well, that made sense. She wasn't part of the club. She had nothing to do. She couldn't take any of the jobs.

That was what I thought. But when the calls died down and there was a lull in the meeting, Laine said, "Are you still going to be baby-sitting this summer?"

I guessed she was talking to all of us. "Sure," I replied. "Why?"

Laine shrugged. "Don't you ever think about getting *real* jobs?"

"Baby-sitting is a real job," said Kristy. "And a tough one. You have to be very responsible. After all, a baby-sitter takes care of children, and children are our future." (Laine coughed.) "Well, they *are*," said Kristy.

"Oh, but come on. Wouldn't you like to earn nice, regular paychecks that you could put in the bank, like adults?"

I was getting fed up with my New York best friend. "Laine, what's the point?" I said. "There *is* a point, isn't there?"

"The point," Laine replied tersely, "is that I got a real job for the summer."

"Your boss has my sympathies," muttered Kristy.

I shot Kristy a Look. Then I said to Laine, "What job?"

"I'm going to run the cash register in Flowers and Bows."

"What's Flowers and Bows?" asked Claud.

"It is *the* trendiest boutique on the Upper West Side. About a million people applied for the job. And Mr. Kellner chose me. I'll be earning a regular salary and getting a paycheck."

Well, thanks a lot, I thought. Thank you for making me feel about two inches tall, Laine. I really appreciate it.

During most of this conversation, Jessi and Mal had been poring over the club notebook, rereading recent entries. It was Jessi who suddenly cried, "Oh!" and began to giggle. She clapped her hand over her mouth.

Mal elbowed her. "Shh!" she hissed.

But Kristy said, "What is it, Jessi?"

Jessi put her hand back in her lap. "I just realized something," she said. "Nicky Pike says he has a crush on a girl in second grade. And Carolyn Arnold says she has a crush on an older boy, a third-grader, who'll be at the Valentine Masquerade. I bet they like *each other*, but they don't know it yet. Isn't that adorable?"

"Oh, wow!" exclaimed Claudia.

"That's great!" I added. "Boy, I can't wait for Saturday. The party is going to be so distant. I especially can't wait to see the faces of

Nicky and Carolyn when they open their cards."

"Excuse me," spoke up Laine. "Let me get this straight. Nicky is eight and Carolyn is seven, right?"

"Well, actually Carolyn just turned eight," I corrected her.

"Okay, she's eight. And you guys are sitting around talking about the love lives of two eight-year-olds?"

Kristy wouldn't even look at Laine. "Yup," she said, and continued the conversation.

I couldn't join in, though. I was thinking about Laine. What had happened to us? We were miles apart.

CHAPTER 10

Friday. Laine's visit was almost over. On Saturday she would return to New York. I couldn't say I was sad.

I couldn't say I was glad, either. I wasn't. I was very disappointed. Laine was being a real pain. She never *used* to be such a pain. If she had been, she wouldn't have become my best friend. Who makes friends with a pain?

I wanted the old Laine back. The Laine I could count on. The Laine who liked to baby-sit. The Laine I could talk with on the phone for two hours, call back, and talk with for another two hours. The Laine who laughed at jokes and joked with my friends.

That Laine seemed to have disappeared. In her place was another Laine. She *looked* like my best friend. But inside she was a different person.

On my way home from school on Friday, I made myself a promise. I promised I would spend as much of that afternoon as possible with Laine. Just the two of us. I didn't want her to go back to New York leaving me with this awful feeling about our friendship.

"Laine!" I called, as I burst through the front door. "Laine!"

"Stacey?" my mother replied.

"Yeah, it's me, Mom. Hi!" I ran past my mother, up the stairs.

I hoped Laine was ready for "Girl Time."

I found Laine stretched out on her bed, reading a thick book.

"Hi!" I said. "What's that?" I pointed to the book.

Laine looked dreamy. "Oh, it's *wonderful*," she said slowly. "It's called *A Summer of Diamonds*, and it's about this eighteen-year-old girl, Spectra — isn't that a beautiful name? — who leaves the United States and travels by herself to this faraway country where she falls in love with this fabulously wealthy emir who offers her everything, even diamonds. So she's about to marry him, but then she runs into this other emir who has lost his entire fortune and she falls in love with *him*. Except he's a political criminal, or something like that, and she has to choose between the two emirs, who are mortal enemies. Finally their countries go to the brink of war. What are you reading now, Anastasia?"

I almost lied and told her I was reading *The Joy Luck Club*, which is what my mother was reading. But I was afraid maybe Laine had read it and would ask me questions about the story. Better not to lie. "Um, *Black Beauty*," I said. "Mallory lent it to me."

"Oh," Laine replied.

"Hey, listen," I said, trying to sound perky. "It's the weekend. Tomorrow you go home. I don't have to do anything this afternoon." (Kristy had canceled the BSC meeting because of the dance. Claudia was going to stay in her room from five-thirty until six and take job calls.) "So let's spend the next couple of hours together," I went on. "Just the two of us. We'll do all the things we used to do."

"Okay," Laine said, but I could tell she was going to have a hard time tearing herself away from the adventures of Spectra and the emirs.

I grabbed Laine's hand and pulled her off the bed. "Come on," I said. "My room! Help me decide what to wear tonight."

Laine smiled. "I know. Wear that blue dress we bought last fall when you were in the city. The one we got at The Limited."

"I can't," I said. "I wore that to a dance in November. Anyway, this is a Valentine's Day dance, remember?"

"Of course. So?"

"So I should wear red."

"Oh, Anastasia." Laine sighed.

"What?" I demanded.

"*Fourth*-graders have to wear red on Valentine's Day."

"My mother still wears red on Valentine's Day," I said.

"Actually, so does mine," said Laine. "Maybe it's a generational thing."

"Or maybe it's part of the reason our mothers are such good friends."

Laine shrugged. "Maybe."

"Well, anyway, I could wear this." I pulled a red top and a very short jean skirt out of my closet. "Laine? I could wear this."

Laine was looking at her hands. "I better touch up my polish," she said. "It's chipping. Anastasia, do you have any hot pink? Oh, wait. Never mind," Laine rushed on. "My nails don't matter. Pete won't notice them." Laine rolled her eyes dramatically.

I frowned. "Okay, okay. Ignore my sartorial dilemma. See if I care."

"Huh?"

"Never mind. I just decided what to wear." I hung the skirt and blouse on the closet doorknob.

"Oh, good. . . . Hey, Anastasia?" said Laine vaguely. "Maybe I should touch up my nails after all. I forgot King will be seeing them tomorrow."

"Well, in that case, by all *means*," I replied. "Heavens. If *King* is going to see them. We wouldn't want to offend his eyes with chipped polish. What a tragedy." I rummaged through a drawer in my dressing table. I couldn't look at Laine. I knew I was being mean, but then, so was she. I located a bottle of hot pink polish and was about to slam it down in front of her when I decided to take another stab at friendship. Or at least at civility.

"Here you go," I said, handing the bottle to Laine. "I hope King likes the color. You'll never guess where I got this polish."

"Where?" asked Laine with interest. "Fiorucci?"

"Nope. I was watching *It's All Yours*."

"What's *It's All Yours*?"

I thought everyone in the tri-state area (that's New York, New Jersey, and Connecticut) knew about *It's All Yours*. I thought everyone watched it. Apparently I was wrong. "It's that home shopping show," I told Laine. "In fact, it's on right now."

Laine snorted. "A home shopping show?" she exclaimed. "You mean you bought this polish on one of those *home shop*ping shows? What else did you buy? Fake diamond earrings? A china clown?"

Actually, I *had* bought one of those clowns. I thought he was pretty cute. But all I said was, "So how do *you* know so much about home shopping shows?"

"Oh, from this girl in my class. She always watches them. And she always comes to school with J-U-N-Q-U-E."

"Maybe she L-I-Q-U-E-S what she buys," I said.

Laine didn't reply. I don't know whether she'd heard me. I wasn't sure she was paying attention. The nail polish seemed to be occupying her mind.

I watched her for a few moments. Then I said, "Want to make popcorn?"

"Nah. I'm on a diet, remember?"

"We won't put butter on it."

"It'll ruin my nails."

Not to mention that the polish would contaminate the popcorn.

"How come you're on a diet?" I asked.

"I have to lose five pounds."

"Why?"

"Because I'm too fat. Can't you see?"

"No." I was surprised. Laine is thin. She's never had a weight problem.

"You should go on a diet, too," Laine informed me.

I should? I'm as thin as a rail. All my friends say so. My mother is constantly telling me to gain weight. I guess all mothers do that. But sometimes even my doctor says I should gain some weight. How many doctors do you know who'll tell you *that?* I wondered if Laine was anorexic. But I decided not to ask her. I didn't want to start an argument. On the other hand, if she *was* anorexic, I should do something. I was her best friend, wasn't I? I mean, she was my best friend (well, one of them) . . . wasn't she?

In all honesty, when I thought of Claudia, she seemed like much more of a best friend. I admitted to myself that I liked her better than I liked Laine. And that was not easy to admit. Laine and I have been friends much longer than Claudia and I. Our moms have been friends since, like, college or something, which probably means about two decades. An eternity. How could I ignore such history?

Wait a sec, said a voice in the back of my mind. Who says *you're* ignoring it? Why are you putting all the blame on yourself? It takes two to tango, as grown-ups always say. (You know what that means? It took me awhile to figure it out. The tango is a dance. And it must be danced by two people. Doing the tango alone is impossible. So is arguing. You cannot argue alone. In order to argue, you need two people, or two voices. When someone — generally an adult — says, "It takes two to tango," he means there are two sides to every problem; that two people are involved in the problem.)

In other words, if Laine and I were having a problem, I couldn't blame myself entirely. Laine was part of the problem. But where had the problem come from? I worried over that while Laine worked on her nails. As I watched her, another image took her place. The image was of a much younger Laine. She was standing with her back to me, her arms crossed. We were in sixth grade. And Laine wasn't speaking to me. I remembered why. We were in the middle of that memorable fight that took place when I learned I had diabetes. Laine was not tolerant of my illness. In fact, we gave each other the silent treatment until *after* I had moved to Stoneybrook (for the first time). Now, that's a fight.

What did our fights mean? I tried to tell myself that they were just bad patches in our relationship. After all, Claud and I had hit some bad patches, too. But they had never been as nasty or as long lasting as my fights with Laine. On the other hand, even though people change, friends stick together. Laine and I are growing up, I said to myself. We're different people than we were a year ago. Our friendship should change to make up for that. I decided to continue making an effort. My mom and Laine's mom had a history. So did Laine and I. Friends for eight years (off and on). That's a long time.

"Tonight is going to be so fun," I said.

"The dance? Yeah." Laine smiled.

"I just hope there are no fights."

"Do fights usually break out at your dances?"

"No. I mean, fights among my friends. I hope everyone can just play it very, very cool," I said.

CHAPTER 11

Friday

The kids are so excited about the Valentine Masquerade! So am I, for that matter. Among other things, I can't wait to see what will happen when Nicky opens Carolyn's card and Carolyn opens Nicky's.

Today I went to Dawn and Mary Anne's to help them decorate the barn for the party. I brought Karen and David Michael with me. I knew they would have fun helping. And they did. Now if only Dawn would get off my case. Oh, sorry, Dawn. I forgot you'd be reading this. But you WERE sort of on my case today. Oh, well. I don't know how the dance will go, but the Valentine Masquerade is going to be a smash!

"Thanks, Charlie!" Kristy called.

Her oldest brother had just dropped her off by the barn on Burnt Hill Road. Also climbing out of the car were Karen, Kristy's stepsister, and David Michael, Kristy's youngest brother. (They're both seven.)

Kristy closed the doors to the Junk Bucket, which is Charlie's car. And it is fairly junky. (Or, as Laine would say, "junquey.") It's secondhand, and Charlie keeps doing things to it. Painting it (it's at least four colors now), hanging stuff from the rearview mirror, changing the hubcaps, and so forth. Ordinarily, my friends and I are embarrassed to be seen in the Junk Bucket. However, when it's the only car available, we don't turn down a ride in it.

"Thanks, Charlie!" echoed David Michael and Karen.

"You're welcome," replied Charlie. "I'll be back at five."

Charlie drove off slowly. His car may be a mess, but he's a safe driver. Good-natured, too, considering he drives the BSC around a lot.

"Hey, you guys!" shouted Kristy. She didn't know whether Dawn and Mary Anne were in the house or the barn, so she just opened her mouth and yelled. (Ever subtle.)

"We're in here!" Dawn called back, from the direction of the barn.

"Okay!" Kristy turned to her brother and sister. "Do you guys have everything?" she asked them.

"Crêpe paper and balloons," replied Karen.

"Scissors, tape, and string," replied David Michael.

"We're ready to roll."

Kristy ushered Karen and David Michael into the barn. Immediately, they dropped their packages and ran for the hayloft.

"You're here to work!" Kristy called after them.

"We'll be right back," said Karen. "Just one good jump!" (She and David Michael like to climb above the loft and jump into the piles of old hay. It's sort of like jumping into raked leaves.)

"Hi, Kristy!" said Mary Anne and Dawn. And Dawn added, "Do you like what we've done so far?"

Kristy looked around the barn. "It's great!" she exclaimed.

Pink and red hearts were taped everywhere. (The hearts were pretty wobbly, and Kristy had a feeling that cutting them out had been a recent baby-sitting project.)

"And look at this," said Mary Anne, pointing to a table. "We got the paper plates and cups and stuff yesterday."

"Oh, cute!" The plates were red with white hearts. The cups were white with red hearts, and the handles were heart-shaped. The napkins were red-and-white-striped.

"Well, are you ready to work?" Dawn asked Kristy.

"Yup. Let me call David Michael and Karen. I want them to start blowing up balloons."

Five minutes later, everyone was busy in the barn. Dawn was taping up more hearts; Mary Anne was opening the packages of plates, cups, and napkins; Kristy was unwinding crêpe paper; and the kids were blowing up heart-shaped balloons.

Karen finished the first one and eyed it. "It doesn't look much like a heart," she said. "Just a bumpy balloon."

"That's okay. *We* know they're hearts," Kristy told her.

"Hello?" called another voice.

Kristy turned around. Standing uncertainly in the doorway to the barn was Nicky Pike. "Hey!" said Kristy.

"Can I help?" asked Nicky, stepping inside.

"Want to blow up bumpy balloons?" Karen asked him.

"Sure!"

Nicky strode across the barn, and Kristy glanced at Dawn and Mary Anne. My friends hid smiles. Nicky seemed awfully excited about the party. Kristy imagined that over at the Arnolds' house, Carolyn was excited, too. Saturday probably seemed years away to both kids.

Mary Anne set down a stack of cups and dashed to Kristy and Dawn. "Isn't Nicky adorable?" she asked.

"Yeah," Kristy answered, looking fondly at him.

"I wonder what eight-year-olds *do* when they like each other," mused Dawn. "They can't exactly date."

"Maybe they date, but they go to the toy store and the playground. Stuff like that," suggested Mary Anne.

Kristy and Dawn grinned.

My friends separated and worked quietly for several minutes.

Then Kristy announced, "By the way, Bart and I are going to the dance tonight after all."

"You are?" exclaimed Mary Anne. "How come you didn't tell me sooner?"

"I just found out," Kristy replied. "Bart called when I got home from school today. Besides, I'm still mad at him."

"Oh, no," said Dawn, with a groan.

"Well, I have a right to be. You don't tell

someone you'll take them to a dance and then say, well, maybe you can't, after all, and leave the person hanging until the day of the dance."

"The important thing is that you're going," said Dawn.

"I guess." Kristy turned to Mary Anne. "You and Logan are still going, aren't you?" she asked her.

"Yeah." Mary Anne sounded as excited as if she were facing a visit to the dentist.

"Oh, *please,* you two," begged Dawn. "Take it easy tonight. All right? No fighting. This evening's supposed to be fun."

"Right," agreed Kristy.

"Right," agreed Mary Anne.

"Thank you."

My friends returned to their decorating.

At about the same time, I was watching Laine paint her nails. By five-thirty, when a BSC meeting should have been starting, Laine and I were dressing for the dance.

"I wonder what Pete will wear," Laine called from the guest room.

"A suit," I replied.

"Really?"

"Well, yeah. *You're* getting dressed up."

"I know, but when I get dressed up, King usually wears . . ."

I didn't care what King usually wore. I didn't interrupt Laine, though. I just tuned her out. However, when she was done talking I said, "Laine? Be nice to Pete tonight." (I knew I sounded like a mother, but I couldn't help it. It was obvious that Laine was still comparing Pete to King — and that Pete would never compare favorably.)

"What?" Laine yelled.

"Nothing."

A minute later, Laine entered my room. "How do I look?" she asked.

"Terrific!" I exclaimed. Pete was going to be blown away. Laine was dressed in black from head to toe. Black leotard, long black jacket, black leggings over black stockings, black shoes. Her jewelry was silver, though. And big. I examined her earrings.

"Did I give you those?" I asked.

Laine nodded. "Yup. For my birthday. I wear them all the time."

"You do?" I grinned. "That's really nice."

"You know what else I wear all the time?"

"What?"

"The earrings you asked Claud to make for me. The tropical fish."

For a moment, I just looked at Laine. Then, impulsively, I hugged her.

"Thanks, Stace," she said. "What was that for?"

I shrugged and mumbled something about being friends.

Not much later, after a quick and early dinner, Mom was standing in the kitchen, eyeing Laine and me. "Well, you both look gorgeous," she said. "And at least fifteen years old."

"Oh, Mom," I said, laughing.

Laine seemed solemn. "People tell me I could be eighteen."

Pretty impressive, I thought. But Mom replied, "You'll have plenty of time to be eighteen five years from now, honey. Why don't you just enjoy being thirteen?"

"Yeah. Why cut five years out of your life?" I added.

Laine shrugged.

"Okay. Everybody ready?" asked Mom.

"I think so," I replied, heading for the hall closet. "Here's your coat, Laine. Let's go. I want to beat the crush at the door."

Laine reached for her coat, but she didn't put it on. She snagged me by the elbow and pulled me around a corner and into the laundry room. "Are we picking up the boys?" she whispered. She looked horrified.

"No. We're meeting them at the dance."

"We're *what*?"

"Meeting them at school."

"Oh, Anastasia. That is so immature. The

boys are supposed to *pick us up. In their cars.*"

"The boys," I replied, my jaw clenched, "can't drive. . . . Neither can King, for that matter. And quit calling me Anastasia. My name is Stacey."

"Sor-*reee*," said Laine.

"Okay, Mom. We're ready," I said.

The three of us left the house and climbed into the car. Mom drove to Stoneybrook Middle School.

Laine and I didn't say a word to each other the entire way.

CHAPTER 12

Mom stopped the car by the entrance to the SMS gym. I glanced sideways at her, then over my shoulder at Laine in the backseat. Drawing in my breath, I made a decision. I had a choice that evening. (So did Laine.) I could act mature and rational, try to enjoy myself, and be adult around Austin Bentley, who was, after all, a friend of mine and had no idea what was going on between Laine and me.

Or I could be an immature brat.

I opted for the first choice.

I stretched a smile across my face and said, a little too cheerfully, "Thanks, Mom. We'll see you at ten o'clock, okay?"

Mom smiled back, looking relieved. (She knew something was wrong between Laine and me, but she wasn't sure what.) "Ten o'clock," she repeated.

101

"Come on, Laine," I said. I opened the door and slid out.

Laine followed me, mumbling, "Thank you, Mrs. McGill."

We walked toward the doorway as Mom drove off.

"Yo, Stacey!" someone yelled.

Laine looked around, mortified.

But I brightened. I knew of only one person with enough nerve to shout, "Yo, Stacey!" on the way to a fancy dance. "Kristy?" I called.

"I'm over here!" She was standing near the entryway, Bart next to her, his arm across her shoulders, and she was smiling. Also, she was wearing an actual dress. Not a *dressy* dress, but a dress nevertheless. She looked terrific.

Obviously, she and Bart were getting along fine. They were one couple I wouldn't have to worry about that night. Now, if only Mary Anne and Logan and Mal and Ben could get along as well.

I hurried to Kristy. "You look wonderful!" I exclaimed.

"Thanks," she replied. "I guess we're the first ones here."

My friends and I (all seven of us, plus our dates) had decided to meet at the door and then go to the dance in a pack. Sometimes we like to stick together that way.

The others arrived one or two at a time:

Dawn and Mary Anne, Logan and Ben. Last to arrive were Pete and Austin.

"There they are!" I called, when I saw Mr. Black's car pull into the parking lot. The back door opened and out tumbled Pete and Austin. As I had predicted, Pete was wearing a suit. So was Austin. Both were sporting red carnations and carrying corsage boxes.

"Ooh," I said softly. "Claud, look. I think they brought flowers."

Sure enough, when Austin and Pete reached Laine and me, they offered the boxes to us.

"Thank you," I said breathily. I untied the pink ribbon while my friends crowded in to watch. Then I opened the box and found a red-and-white wrist corsage. Austin lifted it out and slipped it over my hand. If I do say so myself, it looked quite nice with the red blouse I had chosen to wear. Once again, all I could think to say was, "Thank you."

"You're welcome," replied Austin, who was grinning broadly.

Next to me, Pete was clumsily holding *his* box while Laine untied the ribbon. When the bow slipped from her fingers, Pete reached for it, knocking into her hand. Then, while he was aiming the corsage toward her wrist, he dropped it. It fell onto the cement stairs and was quickly trampled by a group of kids running into the gym.

When the kids had gone by, we looked at the smashed flowers.

"Oops," said Pete.

Laine waved him away, as if neither the corsage nor Pete was of any importance to her whatsoever. As we walked into the gym, she whispered to me, "You didn't say what a klutz he is."

"My mistake," I muttered. But I was thinking, I didn't realize you'd make him so nervous, Laine.

The inside of the gym looked nothing like a gym. It sparkled. Pink hearts and silver rain were suspended from the ceiling. Pink streamers ran from one side of the room to the other.

"My, isn't this . . . pink," said Logan, and we laughed.

"I think it's beautiful," commented Mary Anne.

"So do I," I said.

"It's beautiful if you're two years old."

"Laine, shut up," I snapped, forgetting the decision I'd made. "Hey, Claud, great earrings. I just noticed them."

"Thanks." Claud was frowning, wondering what was going on.

"So who's playing tonight?" asked Bart. (He's a member of a band, and he's always interested in his competition.)

"I'm not sure," said Kristy.

In fact, none of us was sure. Moments later, the music started.

"Hey, it's just a tape!" exclaimed Laine, dismayed.

"Well, a band is setting up," said Austin. "I can see them. I guess this is just to give us something to dance to until the live music starts. Want to dance, Stacey?"

"Sure," I replied. At the same time, I checked Mary Anne to see if this reference to dancing had any effect on her.

She looked a little pale. But that was before Logan said, "Let's get something to eat, Mary Anne."

Then she relaxed. So far so good.

Austin and I moved to an empty area in the gym and began to dance. Out of the corner of my eye, I caught sight of Pete and Laine. They were dancing, too. I guess Pete didn't want to get too far from Laine. Then I caught sight of something else. Pete's feet.

He was wearing sneakers with his suit.

I'd forgotten about Pete and his sneakers. He almost always wears them. When I thought about it, I wasn't sure I'd ever seen him without them. They're Pete's trademark. My friends and I are so used to them I hardly notice them anymore. They're just part of Pete.

Laine noticed the sneakers at the same time

I did. To her credit, she didn't say anything. But she looked horrified — as if she'd just seen a worm crawl out of one of the laceholes.

The expression on her face was hard to miss. It may have been what prompted Pete to say, "So my mom and dad are building an addition on our house. Another wing actually." I think he felt he had to say *some*thing, had to start a conversation. "It's going to have a rec room and a bathroom downstairs, and a bedroom and a bathroom upstairs. I mean, downstairs will just be a *half* bathroom, but upstairs will be a *full* bathroom. You know the difference, right? A half bath has no tub. And right now my parents are choosing tiles — "

"Excuse me, Pete?" said Laine.

" — for the floors. My dad wants white ones with those black speckles for the upstairs bath, and plain blue ones for — "

"Pete?"

" — downstairs, but my mom wants pink and yellow upstairs and these little flower tiles downstairs, but they can't make a decision because there's all this plaster dust, and it covers everything, you know? Even the tile samples. Have you — "

"Pete!"

" — ever *breathed in* plaster dust? It kind of gets caught in your throat. And it makes your mouth feel like the desert."

"Ow!" yelled Laine. "You just stepped on my foot."

So that was how the dance started off.

Here are a few things that happened during the next hour:

A kid spilled a drink *near* Laine. Nothing splashed on her. Not one drop. But she tore herself away from Pete long enough to hiss to me, "*That* is exactly why sixth-graders should not attend a dance with older kids. They have absolutely no muscle control."

I gave Laine a Look. "*Jessi* is in sixth grade," was all I had to say. Laine got the point.

The band began to play. Laine didn't like their music.

Pete brought Laine some refreshments — a cup of punch and a heart-shaped cookie. Laine ate the food, but not until she'd made sure Pete knew she thought it looked more appropriate for kindergarten snacktime than a middle school dance.

Around nine o'clock, the band took a break. Someone slipped a slow song into the cassette player. "Ahh, canned music," said Laine, as if the band had offended her.

"Want to dance?" asked Pete hopefully.

"Nah. I'm tired."

"Okay. We'll sit this one out."

Pete guided Laine off the dance floor. They squeezed between the people in the crowd. Halfway to the (kindergarten) refreshment table, this really cute guy tapped Laine on the shoulder and said, "Do you want to dance?"

Laine gazed at him in awe. "Sure," she managed to reply.

Pete's mouth dropped open. It stayed open as he watched Laine and the boy wind their way back to the dance floor. Then he coughed. (I think he was trying not to cry.)

"Austin?" I whispered. We had been following Pete and Laine to the refreshment table.

Austin shook his head. "Leave him alone for now," he said, meaning Pete. "I'll talk to him in a little while."

I watched Laine for a few minutes. She had draped her arms around the boy's neck and was grinning at him.

I turned away angrily. "I don't believe it," I muttered.

"Huh?" Claudia was standing behind us.

"I said, 'I don't believe it.' "

"Don't believe what?" asked Claud.

I pointed across the room to Laine and the guy.

"So?" said Claud. "She's allowed to dance with someone else."

"Not after she just turned down Pete. The

slow music came on, Pete asked her to dance, she said no, then that guy asked her to dance, and she said yes and practically fell all over herself."

Kristy had joined us. "I wonder if Laine knows her dream boy is a lowly seventh-grader." She paused. "I also wonder if Laine thinks seventh-graders have enough muscle control."

Claud laughed, but I didn't. Somehow I had crossed that line between being healthily angry and being too angry. I guess that's why, when the dance ended and Laine ran excitedly to Claud and Kristy and me, I grabbed her elbow and yanked her into a corner of the gym.

"What's the matter?" Laine demanded.

"You are being *so rude!*" I exclaimed.

"What'd I do?"

"You really don't know, do you." Laine stared at the ground, which made me think she might know after all. "You are treating Pete like dirt," I said. "And he isn't dirt. He has feelings. I can't believe you told him you didn't want to dance, and then that other guy asked you and you said yes right in front of Pete. You know, you are *not* better than the rest of us, Laine Cummings."

"I never said I was."

"Oh, yes you did. You said it in a million

different ways. You have cooler clothes, you're more grown-up, you have more sophisticated taste — "

"Excuse me," Laine interrupted icily, "I would like to go home now."

"Fine. I'll call Mom."

"I mean," said Laine, "I want to go back to New York."

CHAPTER 13

"Fine, Laine. I'll call Mom," I said again. "I will be glad to help you get back to New York as fast as possible."

"Good."

I flounced toward the entrance to the gym. I wasn't sure I had the right change to make a pay-phone call. So when I spotted Austin, I almost detoured toward him. Then I realized he was talking to Pete, and I left them alone. I ran into the hallway.

I didn't realize Laine was following me until I reached the pay phones near the door to the back parking lot.

"Don't you trust me to make the call?" I asked Laine. "Believe me, I want you to get to New York as badly as *you* want to get there."

"Oh, I believe you," said Laine. "I just want to hear what you say to your mother. I want to make sure you don't — "

"Lie?" I supplied.

"You said it, I didn't."

Of course, that made me even angrier. I turned my back on Laine, picked up the receiver of the nearest phone, and listened for a dial tone. When I didn't hear one, I slammed down the receiver and stepped to the next phone.

"Temper, temper," said Laine.

"Oh, shut up."

I dropped the coins in the phone and dialed home.

"Hello?" said Mom.

"Hi, it's Stacey. Can you come pick us up?" My voice felt tight.

"So early?" my mother replied. "What's wrong?"

"Laine and I had a fight. She wants to go home. To New York. Tonight."

"I didn't say to*night*," Laine interrupted.

I put my hand over the receiver. "No, *I* did," I hissed.

On the other end of the phone, Mom was saying, "What? Stacey?"

"Nothing," I said. "Can you pick us up now?"

"Of course. I'll be right there."

"Thanks. We'll see you in a few minutes. 'Bye."

I hung up the phone and stalked down the corridor toward the gym.

"Where are you going?" Laine called after me.

"Back to the dance to get my coat, say good-bye, and apologize to the people *you* were rude to this evening. All six hundred of them."

"You don't have to leave just because I'm leaving," said Laine. "And, you don't have to apologize to anyone *for* me. I'm capable of apologizing."

"You wouldn't even know who to apologize to," I retorted.

"I would too know. Pete."

"And?" (Laine looked blank.) "See? You don't know."

"Okay, who? Who else?" Laine demanded.

I stopped my rush through the hall. "How about the rest of my friends, to start with. Then — "

Laine's mouth dropped open. "You mean Claudia and everybody?"

"Who else?"

"Well, what did I do to them?"

"Laine." I was appalled. She really didn't know. "You were rude to them all week. I don't like to use this word, but you were really snotty. That's the only way I can explain it. Then if you wanted to continue apologizing,

113

you could say you're sorry to the band for putting them down. You could say you're sorry to the decorating committee for saying the gym looks like a place for two-year-olds. You could say you're sorry to the refreshment committee for saying the food looks like it's appropriate for kindergarten snacktime. You could say you're sorry to the entire sixth grade for saying eleven-year-olds have no muscle control."

"Anyone else, Mary Sunshine?"

"Oh, I'm sure there are plenty of others. I just can't think of who they are right now. But when I do, I'll be sure to let you know."

Laine made a face at me.

I went into the gym. I found Austin, Claud, and the rest of my friends in a bunch near the door. "Austin? Can I talk to you?" I said.

Austin and I stepped into a corner where we could talk privately. The first thing I said was, "I am *so* sorry."

"What for?" Austin looked sincerely puzzled.

"For Laine," I replied.

"She should apologize herself."

"I know. But I don't think she's going to. Anyway, I'm also apologizing because I have to leave."

"Now?"

"Yeah. Laine wants to go home. We had

this huge fight. We have to talk about things, especially if she really is going back to New York early."

"Okay."

I glanced at the wrist corsage Austin had bought for me. Then I glanced at him and saw the disappointment on his face. "Austin, I'm apologizing for something else. For ruining the evening. I was really looking forward to the dance, and I bet you were, too. I don't want to leave now, but I think I have to. Also, I'm sorry Pete's so upset. He has every right to be. Tell him I'll talk to him over the weekend. I'll talk to you, too, okay? I'll call you."

"Okay." Austin nodded.

"Thanks for understanding. I have to speak with Claud for a minute. Then I'm just going to get my coat and leave. Mom's on her way over." I walked back to my friends. "Claud?"

"Yeah?"

"Mom's coming. Laine and I are going home now. And Laine's going back to New York. We had a fight."

Claud bit her lip. After a moment, she said, "I have to admit that I'm not sorry. I mean, to see Laine go. But I'm sorry you're leaving the dance."

"Me, too," I answered. "Listen, I'll talk to you tomorrow. Austin knows I'm leaving. Tell anyone else who needs to know."

"I will. 'Bye, Stace. I'll be thinking about you."

"Thanks."

I retrieved my coat and returned to the corridor. Laine was there. Just standing, leaning against the wall. "Where's my coat?" she asked.

I shrugged. "With the others, I guess."

"Didn't you get it?"

"No." Truly, it hadn't occurred to me to get it, although I'm sure I would have thought to get almost anyone else's.

Laine shot me a dirty look, which I pretended not to see. I walked by her, toward the door to the parking lot.

"Now where are you going?" she called after me.

"To wait for Mom."

"But I have to get my coat."

"So get it."

"This isn't my school. I don't know my way around."

"Tough." I marched toward the door.

Behind me was a flurry of motion. I'm not sure how Laine got her coat, but she did, and quickly. Somehow, she must have persuaded someone to get it for her. At any rate, just as Mom pulled into the parking lot, Laine flew out the door. She pushed past me and reached the car before I did. She flung herself into the front seat, next to Mom.

I caught the door before she could close it. "Out," I ordered. "You sit in back. I sit next to my mother."

"No way," replied Laine grimly.

"Stace, get in the back, honey," said Mom. "It isn't worth arguing over." She gave me a sympathetic glance.

I had thought Mom might want a peaceful ride home, so I didn't speak to Laine, and of course she didn't speak to me. But Mom said, "I'd like to know what's going on, you two."

"*She* started it," exclaimed Laine, jerking her thumb in my direction.

"*She* has a name," Mom reminded Laine.

"Yeah, and it isn't Anastasia," I added.

"Let's stick to the subject," said my mother. "Okay, Laine, you spoke first. Tell me your side of the story."

"Anas — I mean, Stacey is out of control," she began.

"Let's also stick to the facts," interrupted Mom.

"Okay. Stacey accused me of being rude to her friends. She embarrassed me. Then she had the nerve to call you."

"You told me to!" I protested.

"I did not. I just said I wanted to go home."

"Well, how were you going to go home if I didn't call Mom?"

"Girls!" cried Mom. "I don't care why you called me. The point is, you're fighting. And I'd like to know what about — before March."

"Mom, Laine embarrassed Pete," I said. "She called him a klutz. She never thanked him for the corsage he brought, even if it did get smushed. And she turned down a dance with him, and then agreed to dance with someone else. She wouldn't stop complaining. In fact, all week she's been insulting my friends and me. Nothing we do is good enough for her. She thinks we're babyish. She doesn't like our school, our boyfriends, our dance. She doesn't like our band or our refreshments. I've never heard anyone complain so much. If we're such bores, you shouldn't have come here, Laine."

"You were the one who wanted me to come so badly," she replied.

"I didn't want you. Not *this* you. I wanted my old friend, Laine Cummings."

"I don't know what you're talking about," said Laine. "And I don't care."

"Fine."

"Fine."

Mom turned into our driveway. She didn't ask Laine or me to continue our conversation, so we walked into the house in silence. However, as soon as we'd taken off our coats, she pointed into the living room and ordered Laine and me to sit.

We sat.

"Now talk," said Mom.

"I still want to go home. And I want to go now," said Laine.

"And I want her to go," I added.

Laine stood up.

"You can't go until I call your mother," Mom told her. "Come into the kitchen with me."

Laine and I listened to Mom's end of the conversation with Mrs. Cummings, which started off politely enough. Laughingly, Mom said, "The girls have had a little fight. Laine wants to take the train home tonight." By the end of the conversation she was saying, "I don't *know*. I didn't *ask*." And then, "Unreasonable? Excuse me, but Stacey is not — What? All right. All right, that's *fine*. Just fine. The ten-forty. Okay."

I haven't heard my mother hang up the phone without saying good-bye too many times, and I don't like the sound of it. When the receiver was back in the cradle, my mother said to Laine, "All right, pack up your things. You can take the next train to New York. Your mom and dad will meet you at Grand Central."

Not much later, Mom was parking the car in the lot at the train station. She and Laine got out of the car. I didn't. (I'm not sure why I had even come along for the ride. Maybe to keep Mom company.)

From the front seat of the car I watched the ten-forty train squeal to a stop, and Laine step through an automatic door. Mom handed her duffel bag to her. I couldn't tell whether they said anything to each other. Then the doors closed and Laine disappeared from view.

Mom walked back to the car.

While I waited for her, I thought about Laine. Our friendship wasn't just changing, I told myself. It was over.

I was fairly certain I wouldn't see Laine again.

CHAPTER 14

Saturday began with phone calls and apologies. Austin was first.

"How's Pete?" I asked, after I had said "I'm sorry" about sixty times.

"All right," Austin replied. "Hurt. Angry. Embarrassed. You know."

"Yeah."

"But he'll live."

"Should I call him?"

"If you want to. Don't worry. He's not mad at you, though," said Austin. "He knows what was going on."

"Okay. Maybe I'll let him chill out until Monday."

Next I phoned Claud. "Laine's gone," I said. "She went home last night. I'm sorry about the dance. I'm sorry about — "

"She went home last *night?*" repeated Claud.

"Yup. She took a late train."

"I guess you had a major fight."

"I'll say."

"Stace? I didn't want to say anything — I mean, I wasn't going to, but now that you've had this fight . . . Well, the thing is, I think Laine has changed. I used to like her. Not anymore, though. She's just not *nice*. She's not funny or friendly."

"I know," I said. "She's a completely different person. I wonder if she seems changed because she and I don't spend much time together anymore, or if she would have changed even if I'd stayed in New York."

"I don't know," said Claud.

I didn't know, either. But I was still sure I would never see Laine again, at least not under friendly circumstances. We might have to see each other at some point in the future, if our families got together. . . . My thoughts trailed off. Uh-oh.

I ran downstairs to make another apology.

"Mom!" I cried. "I just remembered the talk you had with Mrs. Cummings last night. I guess you and Laine's mother are mad now, too, aren't you? You sounded mad."

"Mrs. Cummings wasn't thrilled to get that call," Mom admitted, "and then she was awfully quick to take Laine's side."

"Are you speaking to each other?" I wanted to know.

"Oh, we didn't discuss that. I expect we'll patch things up."

"Good," I said.

I trudged upstairs to my room, where I closed the door and lay down on my bed. I felt heavy and like I wanted to cry, but no tears came.

You better cheer up, I said to myself. The Valentine Masquerade is this afternoon, and you are going. No matter how you feel. You will help the kids have a good time.

With that in mind, I got up, finished making my apology calls, and then dressed for the party.

I dressed in red, defying Laine.

What did she know?

My friends and I met at the barn an hour before the party guests were to arrive. "You guys, the place looks distant!" I exclaimed.

"Thanks," said Kristy, Mary Anne, and Dawn.

"You look pretty distant yourself," added Claud.

"Not too much like a red elf?" I asked. (I was wearing red leggings, red ankle boots, a bulky red sweater, and red barrettes.)

"Not at all like a red elf," said Claud. "I wouldn't tell you something like that. Who do you think I am — Laine?"

My friends laughed, and I joined them, but I could feel a heaviness settle in again. After all, Laine and I had been friends for a long time. We'd shared the good stuff and the bad stuff. We'd shared vacations and birthdays, my trips to the hospital and my parents' divorce. We'd shared *eight years*. I was having trouble letting go of that, even if Laine had become a person I no longer wanted to be friends with.

I shook myself out of the fog, though, and pitched in with party preparations. We arranged cookies on plates, poured cups of punch, and filled candy dishes. Claud set up a mailbox she had made. The kids were going to drop their valentines into it. Later, Kristy would "deliver" them to the guests.

"Well," said Jessi, as she finished tacking a pink heart back in place and checked her watch, "the party officially starts right now."

With that, someone called, "Happy Valentine's Day!"

Standing in the doorway were Marilyn and Carolyn Arnold, looking nothing alike, but both ready for a Valentine's Day party. Marilyn was wearing a casual red outfit and Carolyn was wearing a trendy red outfit. They were carrying their batches of homemade cards.

"Happy Valentine's Day!" I replied.

"Where do we put these?" asked Carolyn, waving her envelopes.

I pointed to the mailbox. "Right there," I said. Then I grinned at Claud, knowing why Carolyn was so excited. I grinned even more broadly when Nicky appeared, our third party guest. But I wasn't too surprised when he steered clear of the twins. I think he wanted to see what effect his card would have on Carolyn before he went out on a limb and spoke to her. Feelings can be hurt so easily.

The barn door opened again, and kept opening and closing until every guest had arrived. No one was missing.

Kristy took charge of things. "Have all of you mailed your cards?" she asked. (She was standing in front of the kids like a drill sergeant.)

"Yes!" they answered.

"Great. Then the party can start. I hope your legs are in shape, because you're going to need muscles to be in the Valentine relay race."

The members of the Baby-sitters Club organized the kids into teams for the race. Following Kristy's instructions, the kids ran around the barn and in and out of horse stalls. They yelled and cheered and squealed. When the race was over, we gave each of the members of the winning team a pen with a heart on the end. The other kids received heart stickers.

"Anybody hungry?" yelled Kristy.

What a question to ask a bunch of kids who had just run a relay race. Of course they were hungry. They stampeded for the food.

Karen Brewer and Claire Pike pretended they were at a tea party.

"Yummy cupcakes," said Claire.

"Simply divine," agreed Karen.

The other kids ate and talked and fooled around, boys in one bunch, girls in another. Nobody was nearly finished, though, when Nicky said, "What's next, Kristy? What do we do next?"

"Hmm, let me see," she answered. "You could clean the barn."

"No!" cried the guests.

"You could do your homework."

"No!!!"

"There is one other thing, but I don't think you'll be interested."

"What is it?" called Vanessa Pike.

"You could open your valentines. But if that seems like too much work, you could help my friends — "

"Valentines!" shrieked Nicky.

"Okay, okay!" Kristy made her way to the mailbox, emptied it, and handed out the cards to the kids, who quickly finished eating.

I might add that when they did finish, both they and the barn were a sea of frosting, candy bits, and spilled punch. I saw Mathew Hobart take note of this, then turn to James and whisper, "Now I understand why we weren't supposed to get dressed up for this Valentine Masquerade."

As soon as Kristy had passed out the envelopes, the kids tore into them. Some went off by themselves, others stood with small groups of friends.

I watched their faces as they opened their cards. Most kids frowned at first. They had to crack those name codes. Soon I heard shouts of, "This one's from Haley!" or, "I get it. This picture plus an E makes Buddy!"

After awhile, I concentrated on watching Nicky and Carolyn, waiting for their faces to break into smiles. But each opened card after card quite solemnly. Occasionally they would move their lips as they puzzled over a code, but I didn't see any grins.

When Nicky had opened his stack of cards, I wandered over to him. "Any good valentines?" I asked him.

"I guess."

He held them out to me and I shuffled through the stack. Carolyn's was just a regular card, not the gigantic one she had labored over. A riddle was on one side, and the back was signed, "From ARNCAROLOLD."

"Neat code," I said. "Carol *in* Arnold . . . Carolyn Arnold. What did Marilyn do for her code?" Nicky shrugged, so I searched the cards again and found a flowery, gushy 3-D card to Nicky from Marilyn. It was signed "Lots and lots and lots of LOVE, ARNMARILOLD."

"Yikes. That's some valentine," I said.

"Hey!" Nicky exclaimed suddenly. He sprang to his feet, raced to Carolyn, and snatched something out of her hand. "That's Carolyn's card!" he cried. "I made it! Why are *you* carrying it around?"

Carolyn snatched the card back. "Because it's *mine*. You put *my* name on it. See?"

Nicky looked panic-stricken. He turned to Marilyn. "Aren't you Carolyn?" he asked.

"No," replied Marilyn. "I'm Marilyn."

Uh-oh, I thought. Right twin, wrong name! Nicky had liked *Marilyn* all this time. He'd mixed up the girls' names.

"Nicky!" I whispered loudly. I pulled him toward me and spoke into his ear. "Look at the card you got from Marilyn. She likes you, too!"

Nicky beamed.

Next to me, Mary Anne, who'd been watching everything, leaned over and whispered

128

into *my* ear, "Hey, if Nicky and *Marilyn* like each other, then who's the older guy Carolyn has a crush on?"

We turned to look for Carolyn.

"There she is!" I said. Carolyn was engrossed in a conversation with James Hobart. She was smiling dreamily at him.

"Maybe James was thinking of Carolyn when he said he was going to invite a date to the party," said Mary Anne, remembering Jessi's entry in the BSC notebook. "He and Carolyn certainly seem happy together."

"All's well that ends well," I replied, looking at the contented faces surrounding us.

Our Valentine Masquerade had been a success!

CHAPTER 15

Late in the afternoon on Valentine's Day, I returned home and wearily climbed the stairs to my room. The party was over, the dance was over, Laine's visit was over, and Valentine's Day was nearly over. Not one thing had gone the way I'd expected.

The party had turned into a pleasant surprise. All of the guests had gone home happy, but none happier than James and Carolyn, or Nicky and Marilyn — who had dared to hold hands briefly.

The dance had been a disaster, but I felt I had straightened things out with the members of the BSC, with Austin, and even with Pete, although I had decided not to speak to Pete until Monday, when we could talk in person. He would be understanding.

I'm not sure what I'd been expecting from Valentine's Day, but certainly not the red roses that arrived from Dad or the dangly silver heart earrings from Mom.

Then there was Laine's visit. What a disaster — and I definitely had not been expecting a disaster. The visit was the only event that seemed over, but not finished. Do you know what I mean? Laine had gone home, so the visit had come to an end, but what about our friendship? That was over, too, but it was unresolved. What had happened? Why had Laine done the things she had done? Was she mad at me? Had I hurt her in some way I was unaware of? What did *she* think about our relationship? That we'd had a big fight but we'd be friends again?

I needed to talk to Laine, but I did not want to pick up the phone and call her. I just couldn't do that.

I stood at my window and gazed outside, looking somewhere beyond the rooftop and the bare branches of the sycamore tree. I remembered when my parents used to fight. Before the divorce. I remembered that when they first began fighting, they made up after each fight. Later, they made up after only some of their fights. Much later, they divorced.

People don't *always* make up when they fight, I told myself. Sometimes they really cannot move beyond their differences. Sometimes — not often, but sometimes — a fight means The End.

I tried to say good-bye to eight years of friendship with Laine Cummings without actually talking to her.

I was glad I had another best friend and lots of other friend-friends. Since Claud was around, I didn't feel quite as awful as I might have if I'd lost my only best friend.

"Can you come over?" I asked her one afternoon, as we walked home from school.

"Sure," she replied.

Claud and I walked to my house. In the kitchen we ate some fruit. Well, I ate fruit and Claudia ate a fruit pie that she pulled from the depths of her book bag. We sat across from each other at the table. "Thinking about Laine?" Claud asked me.

"Yeah. How did you know?"

"I guessed. It was easy. Your face gives away everything."

"Oh."

"Have you talked to Laine, Stacey?"

I shook my head. "Nah."

"Not since *Friday?*" Claud exclaimed.

"Nope."

"Well, I think you should."

"Because if I don't, our relationship will be up in the air?" I asked.

"Yes. Remember when Mimi died?"

"Of course." Mimi was Claud's grandmother. She had lived with the Kishis for years. She seemed like everyone's grandmother.

"Well, I couldn't *really* let her go until I had said good-bye to her," said Claud. "I needed to do that. To talk things out, even if I was just talking to her portrait. It was helpful. I think you should let Laine know how you feel about her and about the fight. She probably needs to know. And you'll feel better if you tell her."

Two days later I took Claud's suggestion. I still couldn't bring myself to *phone* Laine, though. Maybe I was chicken, but I was nervous about speaking with her. I was afraid she would yell at me . . . and that then I would yell back at her and we would both say things we'd regret.

So I wrote her this letter:

Dear Laine,

If you are reading this, then I guess you didn't throw away the letter as soon as you saw my name on the return address. I wouldn't have blamed you if you'd done that, but I'm really glad you're reading this. I want you to know what I've been thinking.

First of all, I'm sorry about our fight. I'm not apologizing. I don't think the fight was my fault. But I'm sorry we had the fight. I don't know why we had it. I mean, I know I was mad because of the things you said and did, but I don't know why you said and did them. Why were you mean to Pete? Why did you come to Stoneybrook if you didn't want to? It's not like I forced you to come. I just said I really wanted you to come.

The letter went on for awhile. I mentioned some of the times when Laine had said things I thought were snotty. (Sorry.) Then I wrote:

Like I said before, I'm sorry we fought. I wish we could have gone on being friends, and I'll miss you. Not the new you, the old you. The person who was nice to my friends and who liked to spend time with me. I don't know what happened to that Laine

Cummings, but she isn't around
any more.
      Goodbye, Laine. Your ex-best
               friend,
                  Stacey
        (not Anastasia)

I reread the letter. Then I folded it in half and slipped it into an envelope. I was already licking the flap when I thought of something. I put the envelope down and began looking through my jewelry box. Hidden under a pin made by Claudia was my half of a Best Friends necklace. Laine had given it to me when I moved back to Stoneybrook after Mom and Dad got divorced.

I lifted it out of the box. Then I slipped it into the envelope and sealed the flap. I addressed my letter, stamped it, and even dropped it into the mailbox on the corner. If I hadn't done that, I might have lost my nerve and not mailed it at all.

I walked home slowly. I had thought I would cry, but I found I didn't need to. I didn't feel wonderful, but I didn't feel bad, either. I had done the right thing.

I phoned Claud.

"Hi! What's going on?" she said.

"I just wrote to Laine."

"Ooh. How do you feel?"

135

"Okay. Like I need some company from my best friend, though. Want to come over?"

"Of course. Can we watch *It's All Yours*? I decided I want a clown like the one you bought."

"We can definitely watch it."

"And can we paint our nails and make popcorn or something?"

"Yup."

"Great! I'll be there."

"Thanks. 'Bye."

" 'Bye, Stace."

I hung up the phone and waited for my best friend to come over.

Dear Reader,

In *Stacey's Ex-Best Friend*, Stacey and the members of the Baby-sitters Club plan a Valentine's Day party for their sitting charges. I love writing about Valentine's Day. In fact, every time I'm plotting a BSC or a Baby-sitters Little Sister book that will be published in February, I ask my editor if Valentine's Day can be one of the themes.

When I was young, I always looked forward to Valentine's Day. In elementary school, a week or so before Valentine's Day, we would make folders out of red construction paper and tape them to the fronts of our desks. During the next few days whenever kids brought their valentines into class they would walk around the room and distribute them in the folders. We were not supposed to open them until our class party on Valentine's Day. The year I was in fifth grade, I decided to make all of my valentines instead of buying them in the store. I had a lot of fun, but I was a *little* embarrassed by them and wondered if they were as good as store-bought ones. So I decided not to sign them. I thought I could give them to my classmates anonymously. What I hadn't counted on was that I would be the only student not to sign her cards. So by process of elimination, everyone had figured out exactly who made the cards. But I still love sending Valentine's Day cards. In fact, I send cards for every possible occasion. But now I've learned to sign them.

Happy reading,

Ann M Martin

L. GODWIN

Ann M. Martin

About the Author

ANN MATTHEWS MARTIN was born on August 12, 1955. She grew up in Princeton, NJ, with her parents and her younger sister, Jane.

Although Ann used to be a teacher and then an editor of children's books, she's now a full-time writer. She gets the ideas for her books from many different places. Some are based on personal experiences. Others are based on childhood memories and feelings. Many are written about contemporary problems or events.

All of Ann's characters, even the members of the Baby-sitters Club, are made up. (So is Stoneybrook.) But many of her characters are based on real people. Sometimes Ann names her characters after people she knows, other times she chooses names she likes.

In addition to the Baby-sitters Club books, Ann Martin has written many other books for children. Her favorite is *Ten Kids, No Pets* because she loves big families and she loves animals. Her favorite Baby-sitters Club book is *Kristy's Big Day*. (By the way, Kristy is her favorite baby-sitter!)

Ann M. Martin now lives in New York with her cats, Gussie and Woody. Her hobbies are reading, sewing, and needlework — especially making clothes for children.

Notebook Pages

This Baby-sitters Club book belongs to _____ .

I am _____ years old and in the _____

grade.

The name of my school is _____ .

I got this BSC book from _____ .

I started reading it on _____ and

finished reading it on _____ .

The place where I read most of this book is _____ .

My favorite part was when _____ .

If I could change anything in the story, it might be the part when

_____ .

My favorite character in the Baby-sitters Club is _____ .

The BSC member I am most like is _____

because _____ .

If I could write a Baby-sitters Club book it would be about ____

_____ .

#51 Stacey's Ex-Best Friend

Stacey has a hard time when Laine Cummings, her best friend from New York City, comes to Stoneybrook and acts stuck up. By the end of the trip, they're ex-best friends! My ex-best friend is _____

_____ . This is how we became ex-best friends: _____

_____

_____ . Laine thinks Stacey and her BSC friends are childish; Stacey thinks Laine's a snob. This is what *I* think about Stacey and Laine: _____

_____

_____ . Stacey probably wishes she had never invited Laine to Connecticut. If I could invite any one of my out-of-town friends to my town, I would invite _____ because _____

_____ . Some of the things we would do together are _____

_____

_____ . I hope we'd have a better time than Stacey and Laine did!

STACEY'S

Here I am, age three.

Me with Charlott
my "almost

A family portrait — me
with my parents.

SCRAPBOOK

ohanssen,
sister."

Getting ready for school.

In LUV at Shadow Lake.

Illustrations by Angelo Tillery

Read all the books
about **Stacey**
in the Baby-sitters Club series
by Ann M. Martin

THE BABY SITTERS CLUB®

The best friends you'll ever have!

Collect 'em all!

by Ann M. Martin

More titles... ▶

❑ MG48223-8	#79	**Mary Anne Breaks the Rules**	**$3.50**
❑ MG48224-6	#80	**Mallory Pike, #1 Fan**	**$3.50**
❑ MG48225-4	#81	**Kristy and Mr. Mom**	**$3.50**
❑ MG48226-2	#82	**Jessi and the Troublemaker**	**$3.50**
❑ MG48235-1	#83	**Stacey vs. the BSC**	**$3.50**
❑ MG48228-9	#84	**Dawn and the School Spirit War**	**$3.50**
❑ MG48236-X	#85	**Claudi Kishli, Live from WSTO**	**$3.50**
❑ MG48227-0	#86	**Mary Anne and Camp BSC**	**$3.50**
❑ MG48237-8	#87	**Stacey and the Bad Girls**	**$3.50**
❑ MG22872-2	#88	**Farewell, Dawn**	**$3.50**
❑ MG22873-0	#89	**Kristy and the Dirty Diapers**	**$3.50**
❑ MG22874-9	#90	**Welcome to the BSC, Abby**	**$3.50**
❑ MG22875-1	#91	**Claudia and the First Thanksgiving**	**$3.50**
❑ MG22876-5	#92	**Mallory's Christmas Wish**	**$3.50**
❑ MG22877-3	#93	**Mary Anne and the Memory Garden**	**$3.99**
❑ MG22878-1	#94	**Stacey McGill, Super Sitter**	**$3.99**
❑ MG22879-X	#95	**Kristy + Bart = ?**	**$3.99**
❑ MG22880-3	#96	**Abby's Lucky Thirteen**	**$3.99**
❑ MG22881-1	#97	**Claudia and the World's Cutest Baby**	**$3.99**
❑ MG22882-X	#98	**Dawn and Too Many Baby-sitters**	**$3.99**
❑ MG69205-4	#99	**Stacey's Broken Heart**	**$3.99**
❑ MG45575-3		**Logan's Story Special Edition Readers' Request**	**$3.25**
❑ MG47118-X		**Logan Bruno, Boy Baby-sitter**	
		Special Edition Readers' Request	**$3.50**
❑ MG47756-0		**Shannon's Story Special Edition**	**$3.50**
❑ MG47686-6		**The Baby-sitters Club Guide to Baby-sitting**	**$3.25**
❑ MG47314-X		**The Baby-sitters Club Trivia and Puzzle Fun Book**	**$2.50**
❑ MG48400-1		**BSC Portrait Collection: Claudia's Book**	**$3.50**
❑ MG22864-1		**BSC Portrait Collection: Dawn's Book**	**$3.50**
❑ MG22865-X		**BSC Portrait Collection: Mary Anne's Book**	**$3.99**
❑ MG48399-4		**BSC Portrait Collection: Stacey's Book**	**$3.50**
❑ MG47151-1		**The Baby-sitters Club Chain Letter**	**$14.95**
❑ MG48295-5		**The Baby-sitters Club Secret Santa**	**$14.95**
❑ MG45074-3		**The Baby-sitters Club Notebook**	**$2.50**
❑ MG44783-1		**The Baby-sitters Club Postcard Book**	**$4.95**

Available wherever you buy books...or use this order form.
Scholastic Inc., P.O. Box 7502, 2931 E. McCarty Street, Jefferson City, MO 65102

Please send me the books I have checked above. I am enclosing $_____
(please add $2.00 to cover shipping and handling). Send check or money order—
no cash or C.O.D.s please.

Name_____ Birthdate_____

Address _____

City_____ State/Zip_____

BSC296

THE BABY-SITTERS CLUB®

by Ann M. Martin

Meet the best friends you'll ever have!

Have you heard? The BSC has a new look — and more great stuff than ever before. An all-new scrapbook for each book's narrator! A letter from Ann M. Martin! Fill-in pages to personalize your copy! Order today!

THE BABY-SITTERS CLUB®

by Ann M. Martin

Collect and read these exciting BSC Super Specials, Mysteries, and Super Mysteries along with your favorite Baby-sitters Club books!

BSC Super Specials

BSC Mysteries

More titles ➡

The Baby-sitters Club books continued...

BSC Super Mysteries

Available wherever you buy books...or use this order form.

Scholastic Inc., P.O. Box 7502, 2931 East McCarty Street, Jefferson City, MO 65102-7502

Please send me the books I have checked above. I am enclosing $ _____
(please add $2.00 to cover shipping and handling). Send check or money order
— no cash or C.O.D.s please.

Name_____Birthdate_____

Address _____

City_____State/Zip_____

Please allow four to six weeks for delivery. Offer good in the U.S. only. Sorry, mail orders are not available to residents of Canada. Prices subject to change

BSCM296

What's the scoop with Dawn, Kristy, Mallory, and the other girls?

Be the first to know with G★I★R★L★ magazine!

Hey, Baby-sitters Club readers! Now you can be the first on the block to get in on the action of G★I★R★L★ It's an exciting new magazine that lets you dig in and read...

★ Upcoming selections from Ann Martin's Baby-sitters Club books
★ Fun articles on handling stress, turning dreams into great careers, making and keeping best friends, and much more
★ Plus, all the latest on new movies, books, music, and sports!

To get in on the scoop, just cut and mail this coupon today. And don't forget to tell all your friends about G★I★R★L★ magazine!

A neat offer for you...6 issues for only $15.00.

Sign up today -- this special offer ends July 1, 1996!

❏ **YES!** Please send me G★I★R★L★ magazine. I will receive six fun-filled issues for only $15.00. Enclosed is a check (no cash, please) made payable to G★I★R★L★ for $15.00.

Just fill in, cut out, and mail this coupon with your payment of $15.00 to: G★I★R★L★, c/o Scholastic Inc., 2931 East McCarty Street, Jefferson City, MO 65101.

Name _____

Address _____

City, State, ZIP _____

9013